Guardian
of the
Ghost Key

K. E. SWANSON

Happy reading!
K E Swanson

DEDICATION

This book is dedicated to all of my children. Most importantly, my own two wonderful children, Noah and Gianna. It is also for Corey and Krista who gave first rate love to a second mom. Lastly, this book is for all of the children that I have loved for ten months at a time each school year.

CONTENTS

CONTENTS

ACKNOWLEDGMENTS

I would like to thank my dear husband, Gordon Desormeaux. Most importantly, he gave me the two hours each day, free from distractions, to write the story that I had carried around in my imagination for years. These were some of the most enjoyable moments of creativity in my life and I value the confidence he had in me. I would also like to thank him for giving me the push (and the example) I needed to follow a dream that had previously seemed elusive. Thank you also for being my business manager, my editor, and my promoter. You gave me the world on a platter and then let me garnish the wonderful life we have together, with the fine arts I hold so dear.

Thank you to my father, Ronald Swanson, and my sister Tracey Swanson-Jamieson, for proof reading and offering many great suggestions.

Thank you to my mother, Bonnie Swanson, for teaching me to do what I love.

CHAPTER ONE

He had never felt his heart pound this hard before. A long, hard run, or biking uphill will get a heart going, and fear; the kind of fear you feel when a roller coaster is about to **plummet**. That will get a heart going. He had experienced those kinds of pounding hearts before, but it was the combination of fear and **exertion** that made him feel that his heart might crack his ribs now.

He squeezed back further into the darkness. He tried to make himself small, invisible. A bead of sweat left a line of tickle between his shoulder blades. He tried to slow his breathing. His body ached for the oxygen that his lungs were desperate to draw, but the deep breaths were loud. He tried to quiet his breath, then he began to worry that his heart beat, so deafening in his own ears, might be **audible** to his **pursuers**. He listened for them, frustrated by the **betrayal** of his own body. The roar in his ears, the pounding of his heart, the rasping breath of his lungs; how would he hear them over them over this racket? A feeling of nausea began to rise up in his throat. He knew he had to get control of himself or he would give away his hiding place, but the fear...

He heard the scuffle of feat, the bang of a door, voices; angry voices. He strained to hear what the voices were saying; he could only hear the anger. It made him want to bolt for safety.

He waited. He heard them banging around, searching, kicking, slamming. Their sounds became more distant as the search moved to further reaches of the building. He listened. He waited. He strained to hear them. There were no more sounds. He waited. It felt like an **eternity**. The sweat dried. The heat in his muscles turned to ice. His breathing slowed. He thought that they must be gone by now, but his legs were numb; he felt as if he were cemented in his place.

He shifted his position. He tried to get comfortable. His muscles ached from the effort to remain quiet and motionless. He tried to estimate how long his **confinement** had been. At least an hour he guessed, considering the burn of exertion and the weakness he felt in the muscles of his thighs. He had been squatting in the same position in the back of this closet for too long.

His legs suddenly gave out. He rocked backward. He reached out blindly for something to support himself with and grabbed onto a splintered, slivering old piece of wood. He felt a brief moment of relief as he steadied himself only to feel the hand hold slip free from its place on the wall and **rotate** to a **vertical** position. He felt his body tip backward and his weight land on the wall behind. He heard a loud creaking sound and the support that the wall had offered was suddenly gone. He tipped back into an emptiness that he had not expected to find in this cramped place. As he scurried to right himself and **orient** himself to his new surroundings he placed his hand on the floor behind him. He jerked and let out a yelp as a jolt of coldness stung the palm of his hand. It was like he had touched a shard of ice, yet he knew this to be impossible in the summer heat. He grasped the little object that had startled his senses.

With the small, cold object gripped in his hand, he became aware of the sound of footsteps pounding down a flight of stairs. He realized, as dread jabbed at his senses, that his pursuers had not left the building and the sound he had created with his fall had alerted them to his presence. He froze. His heart resumed hammering as he heard the scraping of the closet door being wrenched open.

He stared out the open door into the faces of two **belligerent** boys. Their faces twisted into the expression of smug **righteousness**; they had cornered their prey. They peered sightlessly into the darkness to which their eyes had yet to adjust. He watched, expecting their eyes to fix upon him as they gained their focus. He braced himself for the pounding he knew he would receive.

Somehow, he realized that they did not look in his direction. They were looking above him and as they stared he saw their expressions transform from cocky **self-assurance** to... fear. The longer they stared above him, the wider their eyes bulged. Both mouths hung **agape** and one of them made a strange, quiet squeal as though he couldn't get his voice to work. They turned to each other; one whimpered, the other screamed and both turned to run from the room.

He heard their high pitched voices, franticly offer some words of explanation to their companions then the pounding of many footsteps.

CHAPTER TWO

He walked up to the park. It was what his father had suggested, when they had talked on the phone last night. "Go out and meet some new friends, Ben. It would be nice to start school knowing some of the kids around there."

Ben was a bit tall for his age and thin. His dark hair was in need of a trim and the slight wave it had always drove Ben crazy as he tried to comb it down to make it look tidy. His wide brown eyes gave him a look of innocence, but through careful study, he had come up with a facial expression that he felt would portray a bit of toughness. He wore jeans and a plain white t-shirt. He wanted to see what the kids around here were wearing before he chose anything that would make a statement.

He climbed up onto the playground equipment , slung his leg over a bar and leaned back. He was making a concerted effort to look **casual**, in spite of the awkwardness that was becoming his normal way of feeling. He closed his eyes and began thinking through what had occurred earlier.

Was there anything he should have done differently? What would have happened to him if they had found him? What had scared those boys so badly? What was it that had given him this icy burn on his palm?

He felt a tingling coolness on his hip and remembered that he had put the piece of metal into his jeans pocket to examine in the light. He **retrieved** the object from his pocket and held it up to the sun. It was an old black key. It still felt very cool, considering it was a warm sunny day, but not cold enough to sting his hand like it had earlier. It was big compared to modern keys. **Ornate** and old fashion; a skeleton key, he believed it was called. Not too special, but interesting enough to add to the shoe box full of junk that was still packed away in the cardboard boxes in his new room.

He looked around the park; the usual equipment; monkey bars, swings, climbing apparatus. The usual occupants were there too. A couple of old men sat at the picnic table playing checkers, little kids playing tag, a mother pushing her little toddler on the swing. He rushed to wipe away a tear as he watched the mother and child laugh together. How long had it been since he had looked upon his own mother's dear face. Three months he calculated. How much a life could change in three months.

"You survived!?" a voice sputtered from below. "How the heck did you get away from those guys? I thought you'd at least have a black eye or two."

Ben looked down to see a chubby boy with white powdered lips squinting up at him. He held a leash which was pulled taut by young black lab. "You saw that?" he said jumping down.

"Un huh. I thought you were dead meat." He stuffed a powdered mini doughnut into his mouth and offered a bag full of the same to Ben. "Those guys are mean. What'd you do to get them after you?" The dog danced around at his feet wrapping the leash precariously around the boy's ankles.

Ben raised his hand as if to block the doughnuts, shook his head and frowned. "I guess I was sticking my nose in where it didn't belong, but I think there are just some times that it's more important to stand up for what you believe in than it is to mind your own business." He scratched the dog's ear and began to tell the boy the story of how he had gotten himself into such a **predicament** that afternoon.

He'd been wandering around the small town all morning. He was not really trying to meet people, like his father had suggested. He was just trying to get his bearings. The decision to make the move had been rather sudden; and out of the blue, Ben found himself a new **resident** of a town he had only visited a handful of times.

He had followed a dirt road up to the top of a bluff and was pleased to find a bit of a junk yard. Any boy would have been happy to discover such a place. There were a number of wrecked cars with missing doors, flat tires and rusty bodies. There was a pile of scrap lumber. There were broken crates and barrels and stacks of old tires. Ben wandered around, taking a mental inventory of the contents of this haven, and then he came to a fence. He looked over the side of the fence to discover that the junkyard was perched atop an **embankment**. There was a gravel pit about fifteen feet below where he stood; and a group of boys was gathered in the gravel pit. They appeared to be having a heck of a good time.

Ben watched the boys for a few moments and noticed they were circling around something that was causing them to laugh and cheer. As he stared over the fence at them he heard the frightened yips and pained whimpers of a small dog. He watched and a sickening feeling grew in the pit of his stomach. He realized that the boys were making a game of stoning the dog. Each boy searched the ground for a rock, and when he found one of **satisfactory** size, held it and waited for the perfect opportunity to pitch it at the little dog. Most of the time the pup was lucky enough to dodge the stones flying at it, but the occasional rock would make contact and the dog would let out a yelp and a whimper. Every time it made an attempt to escape a boy would dodge at it and corner it in.

Ben's heart ached for the little pup and he was seized by anger for the heartless way the boys were treating a living creature. Frantically Ben looked around for a way to bring an end to the vile game below. His eyes fixed upon the pile of tires at the other end of the junk yard. He ran across and loaded his arms with as many tires as he could carry. Five steps from the pile he realized that he could not move four tires at once and had to abandon one. He dragged rolled and kicked at the tires, and it seemed to take an eternity to move them into position. When he reached the fence, he heard a particularly pained yelp and he rushed to set up his **ambush**.

Ben launched the first tire over the fence and watched as it bounced and bounded down the hill. It hit a large rock as it neared the group, which served to send it flying five feet through the air. As Ben threw the second tire over the fence he watched as the first missile hit its mark. It landed with a smacking sound, square in the center of one boy's back, knocking him down flat on his face. The game came to a sudden stop.

The injured pup **seized** the opportunity to scurry away into the bushes.

The boys stared as their companion lifted his face

from the dirt, spitting and sputtering. He turned to the boy beside him and with a low growl, dove at him and tackled him to the ground. As a fight **ensued** the second tire made its mark, bouncing off the head of one boy causing him to stagger off balance and fall into the arms of one of his friends. Some of the kids were just beginning to laugh at the two boys in their accidental hug, when the third tire bounced into their midst knocking three of them onto their behinds.

It was at this point that some of the boys began to look around trying to discover the source of this attack. Ben, luckily, had run back to retrieve the fourth tire and when they looked to the top of the bluff they saw nothing. After a few moments of panicked confusion, all of the boys began to look around in **bewildered** uncertainty. When the fourth tire came bounding down the hill, all eyes turned toward its source. Ben froze. Everyone below stared up at him. Suddenly an angry roar came from the group and they all charged toward a path that led to the top of the hill. Ben turned and ran.

"Whoa cool!" said the boy in the park, stuffing another doughnut into his mouth. "I'd never have the guts to take them on! How'd you get away?"

"I just started running toward home. Then I realized I didn't want them to know where I lived, so I ran off into the bush. I followed a path and it led to this great big, spooky, old house. I hid in the basement there. It was really weird though..."

"Wait a minute." his new companion tipped his head. "You're telling me that you went inside Mason Manor? Are you nuts, or are you just too brave to know what's good for you?"

"Well it turns out that it was good for me. Those guys followed me there. I was hiding in a closet for a long time. When they finally looked where I was hiding, they were so busy staring at something they saw in there, they didn't even see me. You should have seen the look on their faces. You would have thought they were seeing a ghost! It freaked me out a bit the way they turned tail and ran, but I searched the closet after they left and there was nothing there."

"Oh man! That just proves it! Mason Manor is haunted!" Doughnut boy said. "I've heard so many stories about people seeing ghosts there and about people hearing things, but if George's gang was scared, they had to have seen a ghost. Man, nothing scares those guys!"

"Haunted?" Ben said. "You've got to be kidding me."

"No! Really!" the boy crumpled the top of his doughnut bag closed and **furrowed** his brow. "There's this story about a group of kids that went there to have a Halloween party. They say it felt creepy there even before the party began, but then things started to happen. People heard voices crying, they would light candles and the candles would just blow out, they would see this blurry image of a person and then it would disappear. There was this one kid dressed up like a little girl. She was carrying a doll and the doll suddenly flew out of her hands and went half way across the room. Well I guess everybody left after that and nobody ever goes there now. Heck, I'm surprised George's gang even followed you in there. They were probably all just being tough guys in front of each other. Man, I bet they're sorry now!"

"Well, I don't know about haunted. I'm actually kind of grateful for whatever it was that scared them. If it was a ghost, for some reason it wanted to scare them, but it left me alone. I wasn't scared in there at all. It was really kind of cool. I'd like to go there and look around a bit sometime."

"Hey, you don't have to prove that you're brave to me." the boy insisted. "If you're gonna take on George's gang, I can already tell you're brave."

CHAPTER THREE

"Hey, Benjamin! What you been up to all day?" his grandfather asked, putting down his hammer and sitting on the weather beaten, wooden bench outside of his workshop. With a deep sigh he stretched his legs out in front of him and leaned back like he was settling in for hours.

"Just hanging around; exploring." Ben flopped down on the bench beside his grandfather. "Hey, Grandpa; what's with that old house down the road from here?"

"That's Mason Manor. It's on our property. When I first bought this land I toyed with the idea of fixing the place up. It would have been quite the job, but I enjoy doing work like that. I wouldn't have been in a big hurry to get it done. Kind of like a hobby. Your Grandma sure would have gotten a kick out of fixing it up all fancy and living like a queen in there. I spent quite a bit of time checking out the old place, but I just never felt comfortable there. Something weird about the place; it made me uneasy. Probably just the folk lore about it's being haunted. The kids in these parts sure have a lot of stories about the place. I can't be bothered to dispel any legends though. I figure it keeps 'em all outa there. Bunch a teenagers would be in there, no doubt. They'd be up to no good and wrecking the place. Then I'd have their parents after me. Blaming me for their antics. Agh! Let the ghosts keep them away. Saves me the trouble."

"It looks like a pretty cool place." Ben remarked with a glint in his eye. "You mind if I explore it a bit?"

"Nah. Go ahead. Got your eye on it as a sort of a hangout for when you make some new buddies?" His grandfather seemed to like the idea of a bunch of neighbourhood boys playing **Tom Sawyer** in the old house. "Oh! Just be careful. I noticed the back stares up to the attic, on the north side of the house, look a little rotten. Don't go up thata way."

"Okay, Grandpa." Ben said pushing himself up from the bench. "Where's Gran?"

"She's down on the back fourty, picking apples off the trees." Grandfather picked up his hammer and arranged half a dozen nails between his lips before turning back to the project he had been working on when Ben arrived. "By the way," he muttered through his clenched lips, "your dad phoned for you this morning.

Wants you to give him a call later."

Ben wandered off in the direction his grandfather had **gestured** about the apple trees. He picked up a stick that had been lying beside the path, tested its strength and used it as a walking stick. He poked at a clump of mud, kicked some coloured leaves and threw a pebble at a gnarled old oak tree. He sighed. He knew how much he would have loved this new life if it had begun a year ago. He would have loved living in the country, exploring, making new friends. It felt unnatural to him to have this **depression** hanging over his head.

He thought back to the day his mother had died. She had whispered to him, "Keep being happy. Don't let this rob you of your spirit. Your love of life is one of the best things about you."

His eyes filled with tears. He brushed them away angrily, as if they offended him. He took the stick he had picked up, held it in both hands and broke it across his knee. He flung both pieces into the woods and ran down the path as though he believed he could run away from the sadness if only he could run fast enough.

He found his grandmother loading baskets of apples onto a trailer hitched to an **all terrain quad**. The sight of this elderly woman getting ready to drive a rugged piece of equipment was such an unexpected **contrast** as to lift Ben's spirits a little. Just the sight of this wonderful woman always seemed to have a positive effect on him.

Ben suspected that was a part of the reason his father had chosen to send him to Hazelton. It healed him to be near his grandmother, somehow.

"Hey Gran. Can I help you with that?"

"No thanks dear, but you're just in time to help me in the kitchen. If you like, you can peel the apples while I roll out a crust. I thought an apple pie might help to put a little meat on the bones of my favourite young man." She heaved the last basket onto the trailer, then grabbed an apple off the top of the pile, polished it on her sleeve and tossed it to Ben. "I'll meet you back at the house." She smiled, winked her eye and drove off.

Ben took a **tentative** bite of the crisp, tart apple and wondered how women had a knack for knowing he was hungry even when he hadn't noticed yet himself. His mother had been like that too. He cursed himself for going there again. Even the briefest thought of his mother still brought on an almost **overwhelming** grief. He took his time walking back to the house, trying to clear his mind and dry his eyes.

When Ben walked into the kitchen his grandmother had already donned an apron and had her rolling pin at the ready. She pointed her floury wooden spoon in his direction and said, "Good to see a little colour in those cheeks again. You been running around outside all afternoon? Meet any of the neighbourhood kids?"

"Yeah, I did actually have a bit of a run. I met a kid at the park, didn't catch his name, but he seemed nice. He looked about my age with scruffy hair and freckles. A bit on the chubby side." Ben omitted the bit of information about George's gang.

"That sounds like Nicholas Follows. The family's a bit different, but he's a real nice boy. You'll probably be in the same class tomorrow." She handed Ben a ceramic bowl and a vegetable peeler and nodded toward the basket of apples. "Now what did you think of Mason Manor? Do you get a good feeling or a bad feeling about the place?"

Ben was caught off guard by the question. How did she even know he had been there? "I thought it was really neat. I asked Grandpa if I could look around there some more. Everybody seems to think it's haunted though. I didn't find it scary there."

"Oh it is haunted, but I believe it is a **benevolent** spirit in there. I believe I've figured out a bit about that spirit over the years, and I don't think it intends any harm to people that don't make it feel threatened. People only get a bad feeling about the place if there is something negative about them. All the kids that sneak in there, they know they're trespassing and they feel nervous, so the spirit scares them away. In the past the people who were looking at buying the place intended to fix up that house and live in it. They were going to invade the spirit's **domain**. It made them feel uncomfortable in the place so they wouldn't buy it. Now your dad and your grandpa, that's a little more complicated. I think they go into that house with a feeling of ownership and the spirit doesn't like that. It feels that the house belongs to it, so it scares them away too."

She put down her rolling pin and carefully folded the pastry in half. She gently lifted it into the pie plate and pressed it into position. She looked up from her work with a distant look in her eye and spoke softly. "When I go there I appreciate the beauty of the old building. Not the image of its former glory. I don't look at it and say, 'What a beauty it must have been in its day.' I don't say, 'If only we fixed it up it would be so beautiful.' No, I admire the beauty of it just the way it is. How it has weathered over the years. My eye sees art in how the paint is peeling, how the front stairs are a bit crooked. The lovely ivy that grows on the south **gable**, the moss on the roof, it all adds to the charm. I wouldn't change a thing about the place. I love it as it is and the spirit knows that. I am welcome there and I think you are too. I think that spirit is lonely and doesn't even realize it. A gentle soul like yours might even do it some good. Just go there with your heart open and your thoughts clear." She turned to focus on Ben and looked him directly in the eye. With a gentle firmness she said, "It would be a good place for you to go and think about your mother."

He startled at the mention of his mother. Think about her? That was what he was trying to avoid. Thinking about her was like prodding an open wound. Just the mention of her made his eyes fill with tears. He looked down at the pile of apples he had trimmed for the pie, trying to hide his tears from Gran. Through his blurred vision he saw a mountain of apples big enough for three pies. He felt her hand upon his shoulder and the gentle touch of her fingers tucking his dark hair back behind his ear. She stood by him and hugged him to her long enough for his eyes to clear.

"Looks like I should make another batch of pastry. We'll put a couple a pies in the freezer for Thanksgiving."

The phone rang just as he was helping to clear the supper dishes. "How you doing buddy?" His father's voice was carefully, light hearted and Ben hoped he wouldn't hear tears in his voice.

"I'm okay Dad. I helped Gran make apple pie this afternoon. You know, I was doing a bit of exploring today; did you know about that big old house back in the woods here? I found it while I was wandering around today. It looks pretty cool."

"The Mason Manor; I haven't thought about that place in years." He paused and when he resumed speaking, there was a distance in his voice. He sounded **distracted**. "I used to play around there when I was a kid, but a couple of weird things happened and I started to steer clear of the place. I'll tell you about that stuff another time. I wish I were there to have a piece of Gran's apple pie with you. Are you excited to start school tomorrow? "

Ben's stomach did a flip just at the mention of school. "I wouldn't quite call what I'm feeling excitement." He droned. "It's not like I have the choice not to go, though, so I might as well get the first day over with."

"Try not to show up with that attitude tomorrow. Look, you'll get used to it. You'll feel better when you've made some friends. It's a really nice town to live in, and we can use all the family support we can get right now." His father hedged around the topic of Ben's mother's death. "I'll be up there as soon as I can wrap up some unfinished business here and then we can start to settle in together. I have to get back to work here." Ben could hear his father's voice was beginning to strain with tears. "Try walking in with a good attitude tomorrow. I'll call in the evening to see how your day went. Love you cowboy."

"Love you too pard'ner." Ben gave the customary response and when they hung up a tear rolled down his cheek.

CHAPTER FOUR

Ben took the key from his pocket, placed it on the dresser and slipped into his pajamas. He picked up the key again and slid under the covers. He had meant to show it to his grandmother, but the moment had passed him by. He held it up to his eyes then leaned closer to the lamp with it. It was black, maybe cast iron, he thought. It was shaped like a classic old fashioned key, with the head having a large, oblong hole through it so it could be place on a ring with other keys. It had a long slender shaft and the part of the key that would fit into the lock looked quite complex. Both ends of the key were embossed with elaborate swirls and decorations.

Ben thought of the little box of treasures that he had kept under his bed at their old house. It had some shells he had collected from the beach when they had gone on a family vacation to Mexico. There were some rocks that he had collected; one **geode**, lined with crystals, one piece of

amethyst that was the most brilliant colour of purple, a piece of quartz with a chunk of silver **mica** and various small polished rocks that he had bought on outing with his parents. The box also contained a tiny book of famous quotes that his grandmother had sent him, a bear claw that his camp counsellor had given him and a scorpion encased in solid glass that his dad had brought home from a business trip to Savannah. It also held a piece of dark green glass cut like a gem that he had found on a visit here, to his grandparent's. He'd been digging in the soil under the big oak tree and, there it was just sitting in the soil.

He would add the key to his little box of treasures once he unpacked it. For now Ben slid open the drawer of the night stand beside his bed and dropped the key into the empty **compartment** and closed it. He switched off the light and said a little goodnight prayer to his mother before falling fast asleep.

Ben opened his eyes. It was still dark. He turned to the clock on his night stand. It was one thirty in the morning. He didn't know what had awakened him, but he still felt the tightness of goose bumps on his arms. He rolled over to go back to sleep when he heard a sound. It seemed to be a whisper. He jolted wide awake with a surge of fear. How could he hear a whisper when he was alone in the room?

He listened intently, trying not to move or rustle the blankets. After a few minutes passed, he had almost convinced himself that he had been dreaming. He relaxed and closed his eyes. Then he heard it again.

"Where have you put it?" The voice was strange. He had never heard anything like it before. It was very quiet, but he could hear it so clearly. Like the voice was inside his head. It sounded hollow and icy. His spine tingled.

"Where have you put my key? Please don't leave it there. Pick it up. Hold it in your hand."

Ben's heart was pounding. He reached for the lamp beside his bed and pulled the chain to turn it on. Nothing happened. He felt the **nausea** that comes with intense fear. He didn't know whether to hide under the covers or run screaming from the room, but he did neither. Something **compelled** him to reach for the nightstand drawer. He pulled the drawer open, reached in and felt around for the key. He grasped the ice cold object and, though he didn't know why, held it to his chest.

With the key close to his heart, it seemed to grow warm immediately. His heart beat slowed and his muscles relaxed. He pulled the covers up around himself and the key, laid back, snuggled into the pillows and went to sleep.

CHAPTER FIVE

Ben awoke early the next morning with the key still clenched in his fist. He thought about the first day of school and his stomach did a turn. Although he had always mourned the end of his summer freedom, deep down he had always looked forward to getting back to school. The first day of school had always taken place at Kingsway Heights Elementary; until now. Today he was on his way to Hazelton Middle School. Now, as a grade six student, not only would he be in the youngest group of the school. He was also the new kid.

He tossed the key back into the empty night stand drawer and went into the bathroom to shower. Twenty minutes later he emerged wearing jeans and a neatly ironed white t-shirt. His dark hair, though he had just combed it, looked somewhat messy and a little too long. Ben was tempted down the stairs by the smell of frying bacon and warm pancakes.

"How did you sleep? Did the quiet keep you awake all night, city boy?" his grandfather said with a laugh.

"No, I slept fine. I feel pretty nervous about school now though." He pulled a chair up to the table and his grandmother slid a stack of pancakes in front of him. He added bacon and syrup to his plate, took a small bite and moved the food around with his fork.

"I had the strangest dream last night." Gran remarked. "Someone was searching the house for something. It was a key... that's it. I forget most of the dream now, but last night it was so clear. I woke up at half past one thinking, what is this person doing in my house at this time of night. I had to remind myself it was a dream so I could get back to sleep."

Ben continued to stare at his grandmother, mouth agape, after she finished her story. If she had experienced it too, he could hardly write it off as a dream himself. He continued shuffling food around his plate as he tried to reason through this puzzle. Had he stolen the key from somebody, he questioned himself. No, you can't steal something that you found on your family's own property. Who had spoken to him in the middle of the night, and why did the voice stop as soon as he held the key?

"I packed you a lunch, dear." Gran interrupted his thoughts. "Now, would you like your grandfather or me to walk up to the school with you today?" She glanced at the clock on the wall and put a brown bag down beside his breakfast plate.

"No thanks, Gran. Thanks for the lunch." He pushed back his chair as he stood and picked up the bag. "I'll see you this afternoon." He kissed his grandmother on the cheek and walked out the door.

Ben walked along the fence enclosing the school playground. He thought about how the middle school playground looked different from the one at elementary school. It contained benches and picnic tables, but there was a distinct **absence** of the colourful playground equipment he had grown used to seeing at school. I guess we're supposed to stand around talking to friends at this age, but what's the guy with no friends supposed to do?

Ben's eyes traced along the fence, searching for the opening to the school grounds. When he found the gap in the fence he was dismayed to see a group of about ten boys, all dressed in denim and black, who appeared to be standing guard at the entrance. It didn't take long to recognize that they were the boys who had chased him yesterday; George's gang. He suspected they were waiting for him. Frantically he looked along the fence hoping to spot another way in. As Ben began to doubt that there was an easy solution to his problem, his eyes landed upon a familiar face. The boy he had spoken with at the park yesterday was pushing his way through the crowd rushing in Ben's direction. He grabbed Ben by the arm, forcing him to turn the opposite way and walk back from where he had just come.

"You can't go in that way, pal. George is looking for you and he is telling everyone that you're toast. Come down this way. I'll sneak you in by the teacher's entrance."

"Won't we get in trouble for that?"Ben said.

"If we get caught. That won't be good. We'll just have to be careful. What's your name any way? I'm Nick Follows."

"I'm Ben Rowan. Excuse me for asking Nick, but what's in it for you, if you keep me from getting toasted today. Aren't you going to be toast by association?"

"Yeah, most likely." Nick said. "But I thought it was pretty cool how you stood up to those guys yesterday. I was telling my brother about it and he said that if more of us acted like you did, George wouldn't have so much pull around here. Besides you seem like you could use a friend and I just happen to have a slot open for a friend right now too. So I figure if we stick together, we've got a better chance of survival."

By this point the boys had slipped around to the back of the building where the teacher's parking lot was located. Nick indicated to Ben to crouch down behind a car while a **dishevelled** looking woman rushed up the stairs and through the door. He motioned for Ben to follow him and they crept along the wall, through the garden. When they came to a shrub, Nick dropped down to his belly and crawled under it. Ben stood, dumbfounded, looking at the area where Nick had disappeared. A brief moment later, Nick's head reappeared beneath the shrub and he whispered in exasperation, "Are you coming or not?"

Ben dropped to the ground and followed Nick under the shrub. Ben saw the window of a darkened room that was right at ground level and he saw Nick prying it open. He squeezed through the open window and held it open for Ben to follow. Ben passed through the window with much greater ease than Nick had and as his eyes adjusted to the dim room, he saw that Nick was peeking out the door into a long hallway. He turned to Ben and whispered. "This is going to be the tricky part. We have to get into the hall just before the rest of the kids come in. That way we won't stand out in the crowd and George and his guys won't be able to pick us out. If we come out too late, someone is sure to see where we came from and get us in trouble for being in here. If we come out too soon, a teacher might spot us and kick us back outside into the lion's den."

The two boys waited silently inside the dim room for about five minutes. Ben took the time to look around the room and noticed tattered mops hanging from hooks on the wall, a couple of carts with garbage bins and cleaning supplies and brooms of every shape and variety.

Just as Ben was beginning to relax, Nick exclaimed "Now!" grabbed Ben by the arm and reefed on it until they were standing in the brightly lit hall. Two prim looking young girls glared down their noses at the boys and then looked beside the door at the plaque that read '**Custodians**'.

Ben smacked Nick, with his open palm, on the chest; just hard enough to send him staggering back a couple of steps. "I told you that wasn't the washroom, blockhead!" and the two boys assimilated into the crowd that was now filling the hall.

"That was quick thinking." Nick muttered. "Those two would love to have caught us sneaking into a room that was off limits. Keesha and Katie were the teacher's pets in my class last year. They were always watching everyone, waiting for them to make a mistake that they could point out to the teacher. I hope they won't be in my class this year."

"What grade are you going into?" Ben asked, hoping that this new friend would be in the same class as him.

"Grade six, but there is more than one grade six class. I sure hope I don't end up in a six, seven split with George or any of those boys. Be nice if you and I were in the same class wouldn't it?" Nick voiced Ben's exact thought.

"It sure would, considering that you're the only kid I know in this town. I just got here yesterday. I feel so out of place." Ben confessed.

"Come with me." Nick enjoyed the idea of being the one who knew what to do. "We need to go to the gym. The principal will read out the names of everyone in each class. Then we'll go with our new teacher and head off to our classrooms. If we're not in the same class, meet me on the front stairs of the school for lunch. Okay?"

Ben nodded his head in agreement; relieved that at least he wouldn't have to sit alone for lunch. As the boys walked into the gym, Ben came face to face with one of the boys who had looked into his hiding place at Mason Manor yesterday. A look of recognition came over the face of the other boy and a hostile sneer spread over his face. "You're dead meat after school." he whispered and nudged a boy beside him and flipped his chin in Ben's direction. The other boy sneered at Ben too and smacked his fist into his open palm with a resounding clap.

"Oh, man!" Nick whined. "That's Tommy and Kevin. They're in George's gang. We gotta figure out how you're gonna get home in one piece today." Just then a hush came over the gymnasium and Nick turned to look at a tall grey haired man in a suit who held his hand up indicating that it was time to be quiet and listen. "That's Mr. Franklin, the principal." Nick whispered.

Mr. Franklin began reading out the names of the students who were to be placed in the straight grade six class with Mrs. Johnson. Nick looked at Ben with dismay when he read past the F names without saying Nick's name. Ben was relieved when his name was not on that list either.

Next Mr. Franklin began reading the names of the students who were placed in Mr. Weir's grade six - seven split. The very first name he read was George Anders, and Ben soon realized why Nick was so disappointed to have not been placed in Mrs. Johnson's room. Both Ben and Nick were in the same class as the dreaded George.

When the last name on Mr. Weir's class list was read, the students fell in line behind him and left the gym. A boy with dark, heavily gelled, spiky hair sidled up to Ben, shouldered into his chest and knocked him into Nick. "This little twerp your new best friend, kid? It figures you'd pick the town wimp to hang around with. Ol' Nicky here is as much of a coward as you are. Next time you need to run away from me and my guys, this little tub o lard will slow you down enough that we'll be able to catch you. Then look out!" He lunged at Ben as he said the last words, with a crazed look on his face. It was then that Ben recognized him as the other fearful face that had looked into the closet.

"That was George." Nick rolled his eyes as the muscle bound boy trudged away.

At noon, Ben and Nick both settled on a bench in the school grounds and opened their brown bags. Nick had warned Ben that George was sure to be eating in the cafeteria and that it would be a better choice for them to eat lunch outside. Ben appreciated the fresh air and sunshine anyway and agreed readily.

Nick groaned as he rooted around in his lunch bag. "Grilled tofu on sprouted whole grain bread, for a sandwich." He moaned, creating quotation marks with his fingers on each side of his head as he said the word 'sandwich'. "You know your sandwich is bad when you'd rather eat your fruit." He held up an apple then reached for his back pack. After rummaging through it for a moment he exclaimed, "Eureka!" and held up a chocolate bar. "Score one for Mac!" He cheered and bit into the gooey candy bar.

"Who's Mac?" Ben questioned as he bit into his roast beef sandwich. Ben's knew he should be enjoying the sandwich because it was made out of Gran's homemade bread; he just didn't feel up to eating.

"Mac's my big brother. He's eighteen and he has a job at Walmart on the weekends, so he slips me some edible food once in a while. My mom and dad are health nuts and nothing they buy to eat actually has any flavour. Mac has kinda made it his personal vendetta against my mom to feed me junk. My mom is his step mom. I guess when our dad was married to his mom; they used to eat real food. Mac's kinda bitter about the health food thing."

"I guess I'm lucky. My Gran is an awesome cook." Ben rewrapped his sandwich and reached for the package of homemade chocolate chip cookies his grandmother had added to his lunch bag.

"You live with your grandma? Where are your parents?" asked Nick.

Ben nearly dropped his cookie at the bold question from his new friend. "I live with both my grandparents, as of yesterday. My mom died about three months ago." He paused after these words to wait for the lump to clear from his throat. He accepted Nicks **condolences** and continued. "I was living with my dad and it seemed like we were going to try to get on with our regular life, when all of a sudden, last week he decided to send me here to live with my gran and grandpa. He says he will come here to live too, once he ties up some loose ends."

Suddenly Ben felt himself sliding down the bench toward Nick and both of them tumbled onto the ground. They squinted up into the sunlight and had to shield their eyes from the sun to see George staring down at them with one end of the bench in his hands. "Why don't you two losers meet me at the smoking pit for a rumble after school?" George had spoken loudly and Ben saw all heads in the area turn to see his response.

"No problem." Nick swaggered. "We'll be there."

Ben turned to stare at Nick in utter disbelief as George snorted and walked away. "Are you crazy?" Ben whispered.

"Don't worry. I have an idea. I just hope it will work. This is what we'll do..." Before Nick could relay his plan to Ben the bell rang and everyone rushed toward the entrance. "Just follow the crowd down to the smoking pit after school. Don't worry. You'll be able to find it. Everyone will be going there now that George made such a big announcement. I'll be there shortly after you. Trust me."

Shortly after class had resumed, everyone was hard at work and Ben saw Nick approach Mr. Weir. He whispered something to the teacher who nodded and then Nick left the room. He was gone quite some time and Ben began to fear he had gone home, leaving Ben to fend for himself after school.

When Nick eventually returned, Ben met his eye and was relieved to see him wink and smile before returning to his seat and getting back to work.

By the time the dismissal bell rang at three o'clock Ben had worked himself up into quite a state. He hadn't been working or concentrating on the teacher and found that, on the first day of school, he was already going to be doing some homework. He got up from his desk and turned toward the coatroom just in time to see Nick rush out the door with his backpack and coat in hand. Ben felt queasy and his legs shook, but he remembered that Nick had said he would be at the smoking pit shortly after Ben got there.

Just as Nick had expected, Ben had no trouble following the crowd to the smoking pit. As he arrived at the crowded area just off school property, the crowd parted clearing a path for Ben to approach the center. At the center of the crowd was a small clear area encircled by boys wearing jeans and black. George stepped forward from the group and motioned for Ben to come along.

Ben hesitated, looking around for Nick. He heard someone whisper "I can't believe he showed up." Then the same person started to chant "Fight, fight, fight." And the whole group joined in.

Ben stumbled forward as someone prodded him in the back and landed on his knee in front of George. "Come on Benny." George goaded. "Just because wimpy didn't show, doesn't mean we can't tangle. Let's go!" He motioned toward himself with his hands.

Ben took a brief moment to scan the crowd for Nick and when he looked away, George swung. He made contact with Ben's left temple and Ben staggered to the side. He quickly righted himself and raised his fists, ready to defend. George took another swing and Ben ducked beneath his oncoming fist, lunging into George's stomach and knocking them both to the ground. As a scuffle ensued on the ground Ben heard someone shout, "Follows is here!"

Ben looked around and saw Nick standing hesitantly at the sidelines. George took the opportunity to swing at Ben again and once more made contact with the left side of Ben's face. Ben felt the sting of the initial contact and then the deeper pain of the punch. He shook his head, dazed by the blow and tried to focus. Just then he heard a loud explosion followed a few seconds later by papers fluttering to the ground all around the crowd. Everyone looked up to see what it was that was raining down upon them. A hush fell and people started to look around. Ben looked at Nick whose face was awash with relief. Momentarily they heard a deep voice holler "What is going on here?" and a siren in the distance.

Nick made his way to Ben as more teachers and staff began to filter down to the smoking pit from the school. A police car showed up, followed by a fire truck and a new kind of chaos ensued. George and his gang were the first to make a quick exit, but not before stopping to utter a warning to Ben and Nick. "This isn't over twerps. You're both dead meat!"

Some students began to wander away, while others tried to get a closer look. Nick nudged Ben in the arm and indicated with a nod of his head that they should head off. "Looks like George got you pretty bad. I figured you'd use some delay tactics, not jump right in and fight him." Nick said **incredulously**.

"Jump in and fight him?! I didn't have much choice, he attacked me! What took you so long anyway? I was starting to wonder if you had gone home."

"Sorry, pal." Nick said. "It took a little longer than I expected. I had an **ingenious** idea at the last minute that took a couple extra minutes, but I think you'll see, it will be worth it in the end."

"Worth this pounding headache? I don't know about that." Ben said rubbing his left temple. "What was that explosion back there anyway?"

"I went down to my dad's room. Oh, by the way, did I tell you that my dad is the custodian here?" Without waiting for an answer, Nick continued. "I got a few things from my dad's custodial room and I made a quick pipe bomb. Then I thought, wouldn't it be great if George got the blame for the bomb? So I went back to the classroom and grabbed the science text that Mr. Weir just assigned to George out of his desk. That's what all that paper was that came down on us back there. I had no idea it would blow up so well. I just hope there is enough of it left for them to tell it was George's"

CHAPTER SIX

Ben peeked into the kitchen of his grandparent's house and tiptoed to the counter. He grabbed an apple out of a bowl, a cookie out of the cookie jar and the flashlight he knew his grandfather kept in the junk drawer. He didn't want to take the time to explain his swollen eye right now. "Gran?" he called from the door before stepping out. "I'm going down to the manor house for a while. I'll be back in time for supper."

"Okay." she answered. "Five o'clock for lasagne."

Ben walked down to Manson Manor, eating his cookie and thinking about his first day of school. It had been the most eventful first day of school he had ever had. He worried about how the rest of the year would go with a guy like George sharing the same school, let alone the same class. As he walked along the path that led to the old house he realized that it was actually a gravel road that had grown over with time. In places it was clear that there were two ruts left by the wheels of whatever had driven down this road to the house at its end.

Ben reached the clearing and he could hear the birds singing and a lazy little stream trickling along. He took a much better look than time had allowed him yesterday, when he first found this house. It was a huge two story house with a crooked and sagging front porch. There were large columns on either side of the front door, each of which supported the floor of a large balcony above. There was still a weather beaten old rocking chair and a wooden bench, sitting there, where the occupants would have sat to remove their boots before entering the house. The paint was peeling and some of the shutters were hanging by a hinge ready to fall off when the last support gave way to rust. As his grandmother had said, there was ivy growing all up one side of the house and moss on the roof.

The flower beds had long since been taken over by weeds, but there was still a hint of colourful flowers tucked in amongst them. The hardy little plants must have been the **descendants** of some self seeding variety that had once been intentionally planted in the garden. A big willow tree, which had not been trimmed back in over a century, had branches that reached the ground. Ben figured that beneath the **foliage** of the tree there must be a hollow tunnel around the trunk that would have offered an excellent hideaway for any little boys who had **resided** in the house.

The stairs were crooked, but had not yet given way to decay. They creaked as Ben settled his weight on the bottom step. He admired a big spider web, the biggest he had ever seen, as the sun glinted through it. He stepped up to the front door and, though it stood open a few inches, he felt compelled to knock respectfully before entering. The door creaked open with the pressure he applied, allowed him entrance and then fell back into place, open a few inches, after he let it go.

Inside the front door, was what had once been the grand entrance. Ben was still awestruck by the **grandeur** and the luxury. There was a wide curving staircase that led to a second floor loft which overlooked the two story **foyer**. Faded **tapestries** hung from the walls and a large sculpture of a woman in a flowing dress lay broken on the floor. Ben made his way to the smaller set of stairs that had led him to his basement hideout yesterday. He wanted to have a closer look in the closet he had hidden in. He was curious, both about what might have scared George and his companion, and about the small space he had fallen into at the back of the closet.

He descended the uneven stairs and watched in the beam of the flashlight as cobwebs blew in the breeze he created. He passed piles and piles of broken and tangled junk that had obviously **accumulated** during the years that the house had been **occupied**. He was surprised that the house had not fallen victim to petty thieves in the decades since it had been abandoned. He made his way to the closet and braced himself for a scare as he pulled the door open.

Inside the closet, he could see a shelf that was so weighed down with stacks of **disintegrating**, yellowed papers and dusty books that it bent down in the middle from the weight. There were some moth-eaten articles of clothing hanging from the bar and a wooden crate on the floor. Nothing scary. Ben got down on his hands and knees and crawled to the back of the closet. He shone the light upon the floor where he had taken refuge yesterday. He saw the disturbance he had left in the dust on the floor. With very close **scrutiny** he could see a space in the wood panel on the back wall that bared evidence of the secret chamber behind the wall. He crept into the empty space and shone the flashlight around. The little cubby, contained a few wooden crates, but what caught his attention were the narrow beams of light that shone down from the ceiling. He looked up and noticed that there were long narrow holes in the ceiling and the sunlight from above cast the beams of light that he saw. There was apparently a floor vent in the room above. Ben assumed that the key he had found had been dropped through the holes.

As his thoughts turned to the key, a **vaguely** familiar voice whispered to him. *"Yes, the key. Where have you left my key?"*

A chill ran through him, but Ben did not feel the

dread that logic told him he should have. "It's safe where it is." he responded.

"It is not safe if it is not with you. You need to keep my key safe." The **disembodied** voice **implored**. *"You need to keep watch over my precious key."*

CHAPTER SEVEN

Ben walked up the street nearing the school; his thoughts were on his visit to the manor the previous day. He rubbed the key in his pocket and thought about the voice that had spoken to him. Was the voice in his head, or would someone else hear it if they were in the room when it spoke? Was he imagining the whole thing? He knew he felt good about his decision to put the key in his pocket earlier that morning. He knew that even though the key could not protect him from George, he felt braver going to school with it in his pocket.

Ben heard footsteps slapping the pavement behind him then Nick ran up beside him and patted him on the back. "Whoa! Cool **shiner**." Nick said, stuffing the last bite of a Pop Tart into his mouth. "What did your grandparents say about that?"

"They were a little upset, but grandparents are way

more laid back about that kinda stuff than parents are. Grandpa said he would talk to Mr. Franklin if I wanted, but of course I said no. Gran just sighed and said something about boys."

They walked into the school grounds with no **obstruction** this morning. George's buddies were spread all around the yard doing various things. "George must be taking the day off or something." Nick said. "If he were here his **cronies** would all be gathered around him. I know how we can find out what's going on. That's 'Nora know it all' over there. She knows all the gossip. Let's go talk to her."

The boys walked over to Nora and her friends in time to hear her telling them about Robin Black's missing dog. "They had only had that dog for a couple of months." Nora glanced around her audience. "It was a pure breed Jack Russell Terrier. Robin is so upset. A bunch of her friends are going to help her search the neighbourhood after school today."

"Hey Nora." Nick stepped up to the group. "This is my friend Ben. What do you know about George? Is he here today?"

"Hi Ben, nice to meet you. I guess Nick's told you that I'm the one in the know around here. You need info, I got it. All I ask is that whenever you hear a good piece of gossip, you tell me first. You help me out, I'll help you out. They don't call me 'Know it all Nora' for nothing."

She turned back to Nick, "George is here today." she paused for effect. "Mr. Franklin came out and found him five minutes ago. Brought him into the office for **interrogation**. Word is that he is under suspicion for that explosion that happened at the smoking pit." She turned back to Ben. "Will you answer some questions about the fight yesterday and your black eye? People will want to know."

"Sure." he said, looking to Nick for **confirmation** that he had given the right answer. Nick gave a slight nod and Ben proceeded to answer Nora's questions.

As they walked away from Nora, Nick smiled and said, "It must have worked; my trick with the science book!"

The boys had a laugh together then Ben turned to Nick and asked, "Do you know what a Jack Russell Terrier looks like? I wonder if that dog I saw those guys with was the one that went missing."

"I thought of that too, but I don't really know what that kind of dog looks like. Maybe we should look it up on the internet later."

Ten minutes after class began, George walked in. He slammed his books down on his desk and slouched down into his seat. "Where have you been Mr. Anders." Mr. Weir demanded.

"I was in the office getting the blame for something I

didn't do." George grumbled, then turned and glared at Nick.

At lunch time Nicholas and Ben walked outside with their backpacks and sat on a bench. Ben bit into his sandwich right away, but Nick pealed back his bread and groaned. "Tomato and bean sprouts; how does she expect anyone to eat this stuff." He dug around in his backpack and pulled his hand out with a **triumphant** cheer. He waved a five dollar bill in the air and exclaimed, "Mac comes through for me again! Let's go in to the cafeteria. I heard George has detention for the rest of the week." Nick slam dunked his sandwich into the garbage can as they walked by.

In the cafeteria Ben leaned on a railing and continued to eat his sandwich while Nick joined a long line to buy food. Ben watched as he placed chocolate milk, a bag of chips and a slice of pizza on his tray and picked at the pepperoni as he waited to pay. Ben's attention was averted when he felt a cool tingle on his thigh. He squirmed as the coldness slid down his leg. The key! Ben felt alarmed at the thought of losing it. He bent down and lifted his pant leg only to find it safely nestled in his shoe. As he took hold of the key he heard a distinctly sloppy splat and a gasp from the students in the area. Ben stood up and found himself face to face with a white haired and bearded man in a shirt and tie. His face was dripping with what appeared to be mashed potatoes and gravy. The mass of the food had stuck to the teacher's beard and at that moment slid down his beard onto his tie. A few people groaned and oohed, but Ben heard a voice right behind him say, "Oh, no!"

Ben turned around to see a boy dressed in denim and black with a **sheepish** look on his face take a few steps backward, then turn to run. A hand reached out past Ben and grabbed the culprit before he could escape and the cafeteria went silent. "What do you think you're doing, Colin?" shouted the angry teacher. He held the offending student by the scruff of his neck with one hand and wiped his glasses off on his soiled shirt with the other. He then proceeded to march Colin out of the cafeteria, his determined footsteps making their **destination** obvious.

As the usual **ruckus** returned to the room, Nick **sidled** up beside Ben and asked, "How did you know to bend down right at that moment? That was so cool! You couldn't have timed it better if you had had a conductor!"

"Just lucky, I guess." Ben gripped the key tightly in his palm. He felt around in his pocket for a hole and was surprised to find none. He dropped the key to the bottom of his pocket and followed Nicholas back outside to the yard.

After school the two boys headed toward home. Nick put his hand in his pocket and jingled some change.

"I've got a few cents left over from my lunch money. Let's go to the candy store before we go home."

The boys walked toward town and Nick pointed out various areas of interest to Ben. "That's the movie theatre. They run two movies at once but the screens are very small. It used to be one big screen, but then we missed out on a lot of good movies. There is a pool hall up here with some good video games, but mostly teenagers go there. I've been in there with Mac a few times, but I wouldn't go there without him. Besides George goes there and I wouldn't want to run into him, especially now. This used to be a little produce market. The Wilson's ran it and sold a whole bunch of vegetables and fruit from their farm. I guess they're not doing so well though; they shut it down in the middle of the summer. I heard my parents say that the bank will probably **foreclose** on their farm. Nora says they are getting into livestock instead of crops."

"That's rough. What is this little shop over here?" Ben said.

"Oh, that's just my mom's **naturopathy** store. It's embarrassing, but my parents are into a lot of weird stuff; holistic medicine, herbal remedies, fortune telling, alternative lifestyles. Pretty much what other people call hocus-pocus. I guess she makes money at it or she would go back to working at the Super Mart. Hey what's this?" Nick said pointing at a sign in his mother's store window. "A missing dog poster. Is that Robin's dog?"

"No that's an Afghan." Ben answered. "Our neighbours in the city had one a long time ago, so I know it's definitely not Robin's dog. That's weird; two missing dogs in such a short time. Would your mom know what a Jack Russell Terrier looks like? We should ask her."

"Good idea. She would like to meet you anyway. I told my parents all about the George thing and she's worried that you're a trouble maker."

"What do you mean told them all about the George thing? You didn't tell them everything did you?" Ben said.

"Yeah. I pretty much told them everything. I had to tell my dad about the stuff I used out of his room. Besides I figured they would be proud of my **non-confrontational** problem solving skills. They were." He remarked smugly. "Except for the fact that my timing was off and a fight actually did happen. Anyway, just try to make a good impression on my mom, or we'll have to start sneaking around to hang out together."

"Try to make a good impression? You try to make a good impression with a black eye! Maybe we should wait until it heals."

"Come on." Nick entered the store. "You'll be fine. Hey Mom. How is business today? This is my friend Ben."

Nick's mother was very thin and pale. Her long, wavy hair was streaked with grey and hung in no particular style. She wore flowing wide legged pants and a purple crocheted **poncho**. "You poor thing!" She exclaimed, gently touching Bens injured eye. "I have just the thing for that." She reached to the shelf under her cash register and pulled out a basket overflowing with little bottles and jars. She searched through it, pulled out a jar and read the label. With a nod of satisfaction she opened the jar, dipped in her finger and began applying a **noxious** smelling salve to Ben's bruise. "Now Dear, Nicholas has told me about your mother and if you need to talk, just know that I am here for you." She had such a gentle way about her that Ben felt that he would be comfortable talking to her, but not about his mother.

"Now what sort of trouble are you boys up to this afternoon?" Her tone became chipper as she changed the subject. "I have some yogurt and granola if you need a snack."

"No thanks, Mom. We were wondering if you know what a Jack Russell Terrier looks like."

"I do." She said. "They're a small dog with a long snout. They're very fast and active, and they have short brown and white fur. I think some have a bit of black too. Why do you ask?"

"Robin Black's dog went missing. Ben was wondering if it was the dog that George and his gang were harassing on Sunday. Does it sound like the dog you saw them with Ben?"

"No; I don't think so. The dog I saw them with was all brown and its fur was longer. What could those guys be up to taking all those dogs? You don't think they're killing them do you?" he asked Nick.

"Those guys are mean, but I don't think even they are heartless enough to take a bunch of dogs just to kill them. Let's get going." He jingled the change in his pocket to remind Ben about their original intention to go to the candy store. "Bye Mom. I'll see you later."

"Love you honey. Nice meeting you Ben. Oh!" she said tossing him the little jar of stinky ointment. "Put just a touch of that on three times a day and that bruise will clear up much faster."

"Thanks Mrs. Follows. I appreciate it." Ben smiled and followed Nick out of the store. "Your mom's really nice. You got me all nervous about meeting her for nothing."

"Oh, that's how it seems, but that is just because she took an instant liking to you. If she hadn't gotten a good feeling about you, things would have been a lot more tense just now. That's great though. Now I know she won't be all worried every time we hang out together. Let's get some candy."

K. E. SWANSON

CHAPTER EIGHT

Ben walked home sucking on a raspberry smacker. He held onto the key as he walked and thought about what had happened in the cafeteria that afternoon. He felt around in his pocket, again, for a hole. How could the key have slid down his leg, into his shoe, when there was no way for it to have left his pocket; and the timing? It was like he had had a guardian angel looking out for him.

He walked into the kitchen and kissed his grandmother on the cheek. "Smells good, how long till dinner?"

She looked at the clock. "Fourty five minutes. How was your day? Any trouble with that George fellow?"

"No, he was already in the office for blowing up the book by the time we got to school. One of his friends tried to throw some food at me in the cafeteria though.

He missed, but he still got in trouble. Both he and George should be out of the picture for a little while. They're both serving detentions all week. I'm going to do some unpacking in my room until supper is ready."

Ben walked into his room, stopped at the threshold and stared at the mountain of boxes that **dominated** the room. Where to start? He chose a box that was front and center of the pile and tore off the tape. At the top of the box was his shoe box full of little treasures. He had originally thought to leave the key in this box, but now he hadn't the heart to part with it. It was becoming his lucky charm.

He lifted the lid off the box and pulled out a snapshot of his family. His mother and father were always looking so fondly at each other in any photo he had ever seen of them. This picture was no different. All three of them looked so happy. How suddenly things had changed. Ben ran his finger along the photo and a tear overflowed from the pool that had collected at the corners of his eyes.

He tucked the photo to the bottom of the pile and rummaged through the other contents. He found a long leather cord and picked it up thoughtfully. He remembered putting it in there. He had thought to drill a hole in the bear claw somehow and put it on this cord as a necklace. The hole making method had never presented itself to him, so here the cord sat, unused. Ben thought about how worried he had felt as the key had slid down his pant leg today. He had had to keep checking his pocket all day after that, to be sure the key was still there. Ben retrieved the key from his pocket and poked the leather cord through the hole at the top of the key. He tied a knot in the two ends, tugged at them to measure their security and slipped the loop over his head.

He felt the key tingle against his chest and heard, simply, the word '*good*' in the familiar voice. He tried to convince himself that he was imagining things. He placed the shoe box under the head of his bed and then moved on to unpack the rest of the contents of the box. By the time Gran called him down to dinner, he was nearly finished all of his unpacking.

After dinner Ben decided to walk down to the manor house. He climbed the front steps and, again knocked **tentatively** before entering. This time he decided to climb the grand stair case that led to the second story. He grasped the banister as he began his assent and marvelled at the smoothness and warmth of the beautifully polished wood. It was dull and dirty, but where his hand had cleared the dust, the wood showed a beautiful **lustre** that was the result of decades of careful polishing. At the top of the stairs Ben looked around. The carpet beneath his feet was **threadbare**, but he could see that at one time it must have looked rich and luxurious. He turned to his left and looked through the door of the first room he came to. It must have been a study or office. Ben walked in and went directly to the oversized wooden desk that nearly filled the room. Behind the desk was a brown leather wing chair that was finished with brass studs. The leather was cracked and **deteriorated**. Ben sat down and tried to open a couple of the desk drawers. They were locked. He searched the front of the desk for a key hole and found one to the right of the center drawer. He pulled on the cord around his neck until the key popped out of his shirt. He tried to poke the key into the keyhole of the desk, but the fit was not correct. Ben leaned back in the chair and closed his eyes.

"I like what you've done with my key." The voice sounded distant and hollow. *"It feels safe doesn't it?"*

For the first time it occurred to Ben to try to get some answers from the voice. "Who are you?" His voice sounded strange in the empty room; too loud and too close. It was such a contrast to the voice he had just heard.

"I'm Alex. This is my home." The voice answered simply.

"Are you a ghost?" Ben felt silly asking the question, but he needed to make sense of all of this.

"I am a part of this house."

"If you are a part of this house why were you at my grandparent's house and at my school today?" Ben was pleased with himself for asking this **revealing** question. He waited for the answer.

"I have never left this house before. Now I find that I seem to have the choice, either to follow you or to stay here. It must be the key."

"It must be nice to get out of the house. How long have you been here anyway?" What a stupid thing to say again, Ben chastised himself.

"How can I measure time? I've watched a thousand spiders build webs. I've judged the seasons by the changing of the willow tree. I've watched the colourful paintings fade to grey. I have wished to hide under the branches of the willow, longed to splash in the stream, dreamed of walking down to the orchard. Instead, I walk these halls; climb these stairs, sit in these rooms, over and over."

"Is that why the key is so valuable to you; because you can go with it outside of this house?" Ben felt he could almost touch the sorrow that he could hear in the voice. He was beginning to understand a small part of the many secrets this house held.

"The key is everything. It is not that it is valuable because I can go with it; rather I go with it because it is everything."

"Why is the key everything?" Ben noticed that he was beginning to shiver. He saw his breath form a wintery mist as he spoke.

"I can't remember. I've stared at my key inside that room for days upon days trying to remember why it is so important to me. I have tried to touch it, to pick it up, to move it into the light, but I have had neither the strength, nor the ability. When you picked up

the key, it felt the way it does when you finally get to stretch your legs after you've been riding in the carriage all day. I haven't felt such joy in a long time."

"Did you scare away those boys that were looking for me?" Ben held his breath waiting for the **response**. It would explain so much.

*"I felt instantly indebted to you. I feared you would put the key back down in that room. I felt protective of you and of the key. I had so many feelings I hadn't felt in such a long time. I don't know if I scared them, but those boys had **ill intentions**. I felt hostility toward them. That is all I know."*

A thought occurred to Ben. "You didn't like it when I put the key in the drawer in my room did you? It had been hidden away for so long and then I closed it up in a drawer. You must have panicked, thinking 'I just got it out of one dark hole and now it's in another.' I'm sorry if I scared you."

"It worried me when you thought to put it in your little box and I felt very sad while my key was in the drawer. I am pleased that you have found a secure way to keep it with you."

"I'm pleased that you found a way to keep me from getting a plate of potatoes in my face today." Ben laughed.

Alex's laughter was interrupted by a voice from the foyer.

"Ben, are you in here?" His grandfather shouted.

"I'm upstairs Grandpa." Ben said. "I'll be right down." He called. "Goodbye Alex." He said looking around the room. "I'll come back to talk to you tomorrow."

"I'll be with you."

The key tingled on his chest.

CHAPTER NINE

At school the next morning, Ben put his hand to his chest and felt the key for **reassurance** before entering the school grounds. This was the first day that Nick hadn't caught up with him before he walked through the gate. He would have felt much better with his friend by his side, but Alex was starting to feel like a friend too. If only he was a real person; Ben's dad would be proud of him for making two new friends already. Ben thought he would have to consider whether or not to tell Nick about Alex. It might be a good idea to ask Alex what he thought about bringing Nick in on the secret.

The first bell rang and Ben walked into the school even though most students would wait to go in at the next bell in five minutes. He'd felt a little **awkward** standing alone outside so he went straight to class. As he walked through the door, he was immediately sorry for his **promptness**.

George sat at his desk and looked at Ben with a sneer as he entered. "Ah, my favourite classmate." George said, his voice oozing with **sarcasm**. "Come to spend a little time with me, did you? We're going to have fun being in the same class all year. I'm going to make your life miserable and Mr. Weird won't be able to help you."

Ben felt the icy nip of the key and heard Alex's voice in his head say, *'who did you say?'* "Who did you say?" Ben repeated the question, though he wasn't sure why.

"I said Mr. Weird, **dunce**. Are you deaf or are you just too stupid to figure out that I'm referring to our teacher with the clever little nickname that I gave him." George said loudly.

Ben tried to hide his smile as he saw Mr. Weir walk around the corner just in time to hear George's whole rant.

"What are you smiling at?" George snapped and reached up to slap Ben on the side of the head.

Mr. Weir reached out and grabbed George's hand before he could make contact. "It's not that clever George." Mr. Weir's voice sounded bored. "I've been hearing it since I was a kid, only now I have the ability to punish people who choose to show me such disrespect. You just added another week to your detentions. Morning Ben." He smiled as he walked past and made a note on the chalk board about George's extended punishment.

The rest of the students began to enter the room. Nick looked gleeful. "That's gonna make George real mad, but it's worth it to see him make a fool of himself." he whispered in Ben's ear. "You'll have to tell me the details of what went down at break time. Sorry I was late. Mac drove me to school so we hit a drive through on the way to pick up some real food. Mom made egg white and **fungus** omelettes this morning. The Mr. Cluck's breakfast burger was so much more **satisfying**. Hey, when we drove past old Mrs. Thompson's place there was a police car parked there. The cop was looking in the dog house and holding the rope her dog is usually tied to. I think there is another missing dog."

After school Nick suggested that they go talk to Mrs. Thompson about her missing dog. When Ben asked why, Nick replied. "We're the only ones that know who the dognappers are. If we prove it we **accomplish** two things at once. We become town heroes and we get George off our backs. It's a no brainer. Besides, it'll be fun to play detective."

As they walked toward Mrs. Thompson's house they saw a couple of George's gang ride past on their bikes. Colin held a long length of yellow rope in his hand and Mark carried a large brown paper bag. The boys abandoned their plan to visit Mrs, Thompson and ran to the forest path they had seen Colin and Mark disappear on. They could not see the two boys anymore by the time they got there, but they followed the path. Soon they were able to hear the excited voices and laughter of George's gang.

"They're up to something, that's for sure." Ben said. "Sounds like they're having fun. I hope they don't have a dog again. I don't think the two of us could divert them so easily this time."

The boys peered around a tree. "They don't have a dog, but what are they doing?" Nick stepped forward to try to get a better look. He braced his hand on a log that was leaning against a tree and the log fell forward with a thump. Every member of the gang turned in time to see Nicholas jump back to his hiding place.

The gang boys roared in anger at the **intrusion** and jumped up to chase after Ben and Nick who were already fleeing through the forest. Ben was in the lead and headed automatically toward the manor house. Nick guessed as much and questioned Ben. "Where do you think you're leading me? You don't think you're going to get me to go into that haunted house do you? Cause there's no way!"

"Can you think of anywhere else those guys will be too afraid to chase us? We're safe at the Mason house. Trust me."

"I'll follow you to the house, but I'm not going in. I think I'd rather take my chances with George, than have a run in with a ghost."

Ben and Nick were maintaining their lead on most of the gang boys, but one of them was very fast and was getting closer all the time. Ben **veered** off the path onto the overgrown driveway of the manor house. Nick became entangled in a branch and Ben stopped to help him. They resumed their run a moment before the fastest pursuer caught up to them. Ben had an eerie feeling of **déjà vu** as he realized his heart was pounding almost as hard today as it had on Sunday. Just as the house came into view, and Ben felt sure that the boy would catch them, he stopped short, while Ben and Nick continued running. They reached the house alone and, though Ben would have liked to go straight into the safety of the house, Nick stood **hesitantly** at the base of the stairs. Ben motioned for Nick to join him on the front porch , but Nick's feet remained firmly planted on the stone path. Panting **profusely**, Ben looked back to see the gang boys gather on the edge of the forest and then make a collective decision to **retreat** back into the bush.

"Thank goodness." Ben said then turned and took a step toward the door. "Come on." He prompted, and turned back to see Nick take a few steps further from the stairs.

"No way! I'm glad those guys are too scared to go in there, but, to tell the truth, so am I. There is no way

I'm going in and I can't believe you would either."

"It's fine Nick. I've been in there twice and there's no..." He was about to say no ghost; somehow he didn't think of Alex as a ghost, but he had to stop himself. He couldn't betray Nick by saying there wasn't a ghost, because there was. Neither could he betray Alex by telling Nick that there was a ghost, but that it was on their side. He would have to ask Alex before he could tell Nick about him. "There's nothing to be scared of, but suit yourself. We should wait till we're sure those guys are gone though. I'll wait out here with you."

Ben convinced Nick to sit on the front steps; it was a start, and they chatted for half an hour. Finally Nick said, "I should head home. My mom has probably got some form of **edible torture** ready for me at home by now. See you tomorrow."

Ben said goodbye, then climbed the stairs, knocked and went in. "Hi?" He said tentatively. "Are you here?"

"I'm always here." Alex responded. *"Can we trust Nick? He seems fine and I know you like him, but can he keep a secret? I trust you because I know how much you are within yourself. Nick is so open."*

"You knew what I was going to ask you? I've only known Nick for a few days, but he's been a good friend. He's really stuck his neck out for me a few times already.

I feel like I can trust him. Don't you have some kind of ghostly **intuition** you can tap into?" Ben only knew about ghosts from what he had seen in movies and he didn't know how much of that was realistic. Alex did seem to have an uncanny sense of him though.

"I've got a strong sense of intuition about you." Alex paused as if taking time to think. *"I believe the key links us, makes us close. I don't know if I have an ability to figure others out. Perhaps if Nick would come into the house for a while; if I had a chance to watch him a bit."*

"I really don't think I could get Nick to come in here." Ben said.

"Try."

CHAPTER TEN

Friday morning Ben was ready for school early so he went down to the kitchen to sit with his grandmother while she prepared breakfast. She measured flour, baking powder and salt into a mixing bowl and reached for the bowl of sugar in front of Ben on the counter. "What is that Ben?" She said, leaning toward Ben and squinting at his chest.

He reached up to his chest and felt the key resting on the outside of his t-shirt. He was annoyed at himself for being so careless. Thankfully it was his grandmother who had seen it, not someone he didn't trust. "I found this key at the manor house. I've never seen anything like it, so I thought I'd keep it. I wonder what it unlocks. Do you have any idea?"

His grandmother reached out and gently picked it up. "It's so cold!" she said. "It is lovely." she admired it, turning it over in her hand and rubbing it under her thumb. "It does make a nice piece of jewellery. I suppose that is the latest thing that kids are wearing these days, is it? This could open any number of things. There was a time that most keys looked something like this. This is pretty old; at least from the eighteen hundreds; I think. It is very **ornate** though. That gives me the impression that it opens something that belonged to a wealthy person. I would suggest that the item it opens would be just as **elaborately** decorated as the key. I think you'll find..." She reached into the cupboard under the sink and brought out a rusty little tin and passed it to Ben with a rag. "I think you'll find that it is made out of sterling silver. If you give it a good polishing you'll have yourself an even nicer piece of jewellery."

Ben pulled the cord off his neck, untied it and removed the key. He hesitated. It is Alex's key. Should I ask him before I polish it? No, he second guessed himself, it might be a nice surprise for Alex to see it the way he remembered it. Maybe that will jog his memory as to what it opens.

He opened the tin, rubbed the rag across the greyish substance inside and began to polish the key. He rubbed the same spot for quite some time, before he began to see the rewards of his labour. As the blackness **transferred** from the key to the rag, a warm, slightly yellowish, silver colour began to emerge. He continued to polish frantically until the whole key was gleaming. He moved to the kitchen sink to rinse the last of the polish. He turned the tap on over the key and felt a sudden twinge in his finger. He moved to pull his hand away from the key, but found that the key stuck to his finger momentarily before clattering to the bottom of the sink. He shook his hand as if to shake off the pain and dried his hands on the cotton towel that hung near the sink. He picked up the key and examined it in the light. The shine had clouded over leaving the whole key looking grey rather than silver and Ben's first thought was that Alex was angry. A drip fell from the key and Ben moved it closer to his eyes. He realized then that the key was coated in a thin layer of ice.

"Isn't that odd?" Gran puzzled. "I've never seen silver polish do that before." She took the tin and threw it into the garbage can. "It must be getting too old." She picked up a stub of a pencil and scratched at the grocery list on the kitchen table.

Ben warmed the key in his palm until the thin layer of ice was melted, dried it on the kitchen towel and admired its new sheen in the sunlight. He carefully threaded the cord through the hole again and tied a tight knot. As he passed the loop of the cord over his head and the key rested again on his chest he felt, what could best be described as a hum or a vibration from the key.

Later that morning, Ben walked to school with a

feeling of excitement building inside of him. He could hardly wait to show the key to Alex. He did have a bit of a problem to figure out and, he thought, he would like to have a solution by the end of the day. How would he get Nick to go into Mason Manor? He didn't want to trick him into it; that might make him mad. He knew from yesterday that there would be no convincing Nick to go in. Ben had just decided to let it go for the time being, when he heard his friend's voice shout from a distance.

"Hey, Ben; wait for me!" Nick caught up and Ben noticed the worried expression on his friend's face. "I just saw Nora and she told me that George is looking for us. He told her that he has a challenge for us." Nick made finger quotation marks as he said the word challenge. "I think we made them really mad yesterday. We could be in big trouble."

"Do you think we should avoid him as long as possible or just walk right up to him and ask what he wants?" Ben felt as worried as Nick looked.

"Walk right up to him? To tell the truth, that option never even occurred to me. I've always been the, avoid trouble, kind of guy." Nick admitted. "That would throw him off though, wouldn't it? Probably half his pleasure is in knowing that we are going to be afraid all day. Let's do it, but we should make sure there is a teacher around when we do, so we don't get clobbered."

Satisfied with their decision, Ben changed the

subject. "I want to show you something, Nick." He pulled on the cord around his neck. As the key popped out of his shirt, Nick stopped to have a look. "I found this and I've been carrying it around all week. It was black when I found it, but Gran gave me some silver polish this morning and now it looks pretty cool."

"Whoa! I wonder what that opens." Nick touched the key. "Do you know?"

Ben saw an opportunity present its self. "No, but I was hoping you would help me figure it out. Whatever it opens, must be in the Mason house. I thought maybe we could go explore and search the house for things with key holes"

"No way!" Nick pulled his hand away from the key. "I already told you, I'm not going in there."

The boys walked up to the school and before Ben had a chance to try to convince Nick, he spotted George. Ben nudged Nick and gave a nod in his direction. "You think we should get this over with before we change our minds and chicken out. Miss Phillips is right there. He's not going to do anything to add to his detention time."

"Let's do it." Nick said, not looking as brave as his voice sounded. Ben couldn't blame him. The less contact they had with George, the better.

"George!" Nick called out, the quaver in his voice giving away his nervousness. "Nora said you wanted to talk to Ben and me. You need some help with math or something?"

"That's real funny. Like I'd need help from a grade sixer. Nah, me and the gang have a challenge for you." he snickered and looked at his buddies knowingly. "Let's see who is braver. Let's all go down to the haunted house after dark tonight and see who has the guts to go in. What do you think?"

Nick hesitated and Ben took the opportunity to answer first. "Are you kidding me?" He feigned fear. "You would really go in there? After what happened last time? I don't know if we're up for that." He made a quick glance toward Nick then continued before Nick could **interject**. "Okay, Nick, if you're sure. We'll meet you there at nine thirty tonight." He grabbed Nick by the arm and pulled him away.

When they were out of earshot, Nick turned on Ben and said, "That's easy for you isn't it? You don't have the sense to be scared of the place, but I do and now I have to go in there or I look like a complete fool. Thanks a-lot."

He really looked angry and Ben rushed to explain himself before he lost the opportunity. "I'm sorry you feel cornered, but I really think this can work for us. I know something about the manor that no one else does. Really Nick; please trust me on this. It will be great. They'll be scared and we won't."

"How can you promise that? Do you have control over the ghost or something?" Nick asked with a strong note of sarcasm.

"Give me a chance Nick. Come with me to the manor house after school today. It will still be daylight. I'll let you in on the secret then and if you still don't feel comfortable, we just won't show up at night. What do you say?"

"Let me think about it. I'll tell you my answer after school."

CHAPTER ELEVEN

All day Nick gave Ben the cold shoulder. They sat together at lunchtime, but Nick made it clear that he was angry with Ben. Ben felt a little bit guilty, but felt that he would be redeemed after school if only Nick would come with him to Mason Manor. He worried a little that Alex would not cooperate. If Alex didn't like Nick, for some reason, any number of things could go wrong. He might not speak to Nick; worse he might scare Nick. Then how would his friendship with Nick stand and how would things go with the George situation?

Both boys were worried and distracted all day and when the bell rang it was a relief for both of them. "I can't believe I'm agreeing to this; let's go." Nick said. "I want to get this over with."

"You won't regret this." Ben said almost as much to convince himself as to convince Nick.

They walked in silence to the manor house and when they got to the steps of the old building, Ben walked up, while Nick waited on the walkway in front.

Ben turned around to prompt him, but stopped himself when he saw Nick's pale face and furrowed brow. "I'm sorry this freaks you out so much, Nick." he said. "If this goes the way I hope it will, you'll never be scared to go in here again. You just have to trust me."

"Okay." Nick said with a deep sigh and placed his foot hesitantly on the first step. He climbed to the top of the stairs and waited as Ben knocked on the door, then opened it. "What did you knock for?" Nick sounded alarmed. "Do I need to knock too?"

"I knock here just the same as I would knock on the door if I came to your house." Ben explained "This isn't my house; it's the polite thing to do. I don't think you need to knock too. If we both went to someone else's house, one knock would do for both of us, if we showed up at the same time; but go ahead and knock if it makes you feel better. One thing I've learned about this house is that you are better off to follow your instinct. Be yourself. You ready?"

Nick nodded, knocked on the door and followed Ben into the foyer. Ben didn't know how long Alex was going to need to make up his mind about Nick. He hadn't thought about how he was going to delay Nick while Alex made his decision. He decided maybe they should just walk slowly through the house and maybe Alex could make his evaluation by the time they reached some sort of turnaround point.

Ben had taken only a few steps in the direction of the stair case when he noticed a young girl seated about mid way up the stairs. She had long, dark hair that was twisted into a braid which hung in the front over her left shoulder. She wore a pale pink, lacy dress and shiny black shoes. Ben found it odd that she would be dressed up, like she was ready for a party and sitting here in this house. What was worse was that she would probably ruin his opportunity to introduce Nick to Alex.

"Hi." Ben said. He didn't know if she had any right to be here, but it was not his usual nature to be rude. "What are you doing here?"

"I'm waiting for a friend. What are you doing?" she said.

"I'm just showing my friend around the place. It's really a cool house, if you can get past the ghost stories. You're not afraid to hang around here?" he tested her knowledge of the place.

"Oh, I'm not scared at all. If there are any ghosts here, they must be friendly. I spend a lot of time here. What does your friend think of the place? He looks as if he's ready to faint." The girl looked at Nick with concern.

Ben turned to Nick and realized that the girl's

worry was not **unfounded**. Nick's skin was **ashen** and his eyes looked watery. He looked as if he was ready to fall down. Ben rushed to his side and propped him up with an arm. "You okay, buddy? We don't have to do this if you're that uncomfortable."

"I'm starting to feel better about the whole thing. At least there are no ghosts flying out at us. Maybe all those stories just got blown out of proportion. What was it you were going to show me anyway?" He pulled away from Ben's arm of support and stood on his own strength.

"I'll get to that in a while." he said giving Nick a subtle look that said 'not while she's here.'

"You two go ahead and do your thing." the girl said with a little smile. "I'll just wait here."

Ben was getting a little annoyed. He was tempted to use the 'this is my grandfather's property' card, but something stopped him. What was she smiling about any way? "Suit yourself." he said and walked past her on the stairs. Nick followed closely and when they reached the top of the stairs they walked down the hall.

"I don't know if this is going to work out the way I had hoped with her here." Ben whispered to Nick as they stopped outside the doors of a room at the end of the hall. "Does she go to our school? I've never seen her before. Have you?"

"I don't know her at all, and what's with those clothes?" Nick whispered. "Either she stopped here on her way to a wedding, or she thinks there is going to be a Halloween party here tonight."

The boys shook their heads and opened the door to enter the room. They both startled and gasped to find the girl from the stairs sitting on the window ledge in the room. "Whoa! You freaked me out!" Ben stated a little too loudly. "How did you get in here so quick? Is there a secret passage or something?"

"Oh, this house is full of surprises." She chuckled.

Ben's annoyance was growing and his impatience was beginning to show. "Who are you? Where do you come from and what are you doing here?"

"Oh, come now, Ben. Can't a girl have a little fun?" she asked sincerely, shaking her head. "I thought you'd have figured it out by now." She paused looking him directly in the eye as if he should know her. "I'm Alexa." she said **emphatically**.

Ben stared at her, **dumbfounded** for a moment before his jaw dropped and his head **jutted** forward. His mouth opened and closed a couple times as if he couldn't get the words to come out. "Alexa?" he repeated with a shake of his head. "You're a girl?!"

"You thought I was a boy?" Alexa looked insulted.

"You told me your name was Alex. I just assumed..." his voice trailed off as he realized the error of his assumption. "I can see you this time!" he said abruptly."Why can I suddenly see you?"

"I didn't know at first. I felt different this morning; stronger. It's like when you don't feel well, but you don't really realize it until you start to feel better." Her excitement grew as she spoke. "I didn't know what was different until I saw the key just now. You polished it. It looks so beautiful and now I feel so much stronger!"

"I wondered, for a second, if I should ask you before I polished it! " Ben wanted her to know that he still considered the key to belong to her. "Then I thought, what could it hurt? And I went ahead and did it. I thought it would be a nice surprise. Do you like it?"

"It's wonderful..."Alexa stopped talking, looked to Ben's left and tilted her head.

Ben turned to his side and shook his head. In the excitement he had forgotten that Nick was with him. Nick stood with his mouth agape and his eyes bulging. Ben touched him on the shoulder, but Nick continued to stare at Alexa in disbelief. "I think you'd better sit down buddy." Ben said.

Ben guided Nick to a dusty, upholstered chair. "This is my friend Alexa. She's the reason I brought you here." Ben spoke gently and eased Nick into the seat.

"This is Alexa's house. She lives here." Ben searched for the words that would explain what he was trying to say. He grappled to find a way to explain Alexa without scaring Nick.

"Yeah, okay." Nick said. "So this is your friend, ... the ghost!" his voice was strained and high pitched. "You brought me here to meet your friend the ghost. Okay." He blew his breath out and shook his head still staring ahead at nothing.

"You going to be okay Nick?" Ben said.

"Okay? Yeah I'm going to be okay. Just give me a few minutes to wrap my head around this whole friendly ghost thing. I think I'll be okay. Just a minute and I'll be okay..." his voice trailed off as he settled into thought.

Ben turned back to Alexa. "So you decided Nick was alright then? When did you decide that? I thought you wanted some time to feel him out."

"I knew the moment he walked through the door, that we could trust him. He was so scared and he was still willing to walk in here with you. He's really a good friend Ben; I don't know if you even realize what it took for him to come here with you."

"I'm so glad you feel that way about him. I'm afraid we're going to need your help tonight. We've gotten into a bit of a bad situation that I'm hoping you can help us with."

Nick stood and joined the two, looking at least partly recovered from the shock. "You really don't look ghostly." he said to Alexa. "Aren't you supposed to be kinda see through or something? The only difference I see is that you kind of look a bit shimmery once in a while."

"I'm new to this too, Nick." Alexa confessed. "I've spent most of my time alone here. I don't know if I was visible or not. The times that I do know that people saw me, were times I felt frightened. I guess that I scared them away. Anyway, what do you two need my help with?" They stood together and spoke in hushed tones making plans for the night time excursion.

That evening, Ben kissed his Grandmother goodnight, making excuses about being tired, and went up to his room at nine o'clock. He would have preferred to tell his grandmother the truth, but even **indulgent** grandparents have some limits. Ben slipped on his jacket, put a flashlight in his pocket and patted the key on his chest. He then climbed out of his bedroom window onto the roof of the front porch. He tiptoed down the roof to the end of the porch and climbed down onto the railing. He took one last look at his grandparents through the window as they watched their Friday night programs on the TV, then jumped to the ground.

Ben met Nick, as planned, at the point where his

grandparent's driveway intersected with the path to the Mason Manor. They uttered a quick greeting to each other and began to move down the path. They reached the manor house before any of the boys from George's gang began to arrive. They stood outside the house to wait and Ben began to wish that Alexa could be with them; it would be reassuring to know she was close by when George and his friends showed up.

The boys grew more and more nervous as time passed. They had made grand plans with Alexa. After they all entered the house she was going to start making little noises and blow out the candle that Nick had brought. They planned to build to stronger and stronger scare **tactics**, all the while showing no signs of fear themselves; even laughing at George and his friends for their fear. The whole show would **culminate** in Alexa flying down the stairs looking as frightful as she could and chasing them from the house. Ben and Nick planned to call out the door, mocking them as they ran away. This show of bravery, they hoped, would get George off their backs for the rest of the year.

The only concern, and this was what was on their minds now, was how frightening Alexa could actually make herself look. When she had frightened people away before it had not been intentional. It seemed to her, that her own fear had become so powerful as to cause her to look frightening. She really wasn't even sure what had been so scary. Ben had reassured her that if she could do nothing to make her appearance frightening, she should just scream as loudly as she could. He felt certain that, as a last resource, that would do. Nick agreed.

The boys grew more tense in the darkness and as time passed they began to wonder if the gang boys were going to show up. As Nick was about to voice his doubt, they heard some movement in the forest. There was no talking amongst the approaching boys, giving away the level of nervousness they felt. Soon, George emerged from the darkness of the forest, leading a group of eight boys. As they came close enough to be heard one of the boys said, "We're late because we were waiting for Colin. He never did show. Guess he couldn't get away."

"Or he was too scared." Nick responded. He was pleasantly surprised at his own **cavalier** attitude. "What are we waiting for? You guys ready to go in?"

After a few awkward agreements from George's gang, Ben turned, gave his ritual knock on the door and entered first. Nick and the gang followed. Nick walked to the center of the foyer and set the candle on the floor. He struck a match and lit the wick. With great satisfaction, he watched as the candle blew out. He lit it again and it flickered, but stayed lit. Everyone waited in silent expectation. The boys all listened intently to the sounds of the night. They could hear the rasping of their own breath, the scuffing of their feet on the wooden floor, a cricket outside, the rustling of leaves. It seemed a long time had passed when a quiet creaking sound was heard from the front porch. The sound of footsteps coming up the front stairs was loud in the silence. Suddenly the front door flew open, frightening even Ben and Nick. All eyes focused on the door with grave expectation, only to see Ben's grandfather, fumble then turn on a flashlight.

"What in the world?" he muttered. "What are all you boys doing out at this time of night? And Ben, What are you doing sneaking off in the night without telling your Gran and me? You gave us an awful fright when we went up to get you to the phone for your dad. My word! Do any of your parents know where you boys are at," he looked at his watch, "ten o'clock at night?"

"Sorry Mr. Rowan. Ben had something he wanted to show us here. We thought you knew we were coming." As the other boys began to move around a bit and talk, George faked an accidental bump into Ben, digging his elbow painfully into Ben's ribs. "Made plans for gramps to come rescue you huh? You little coward." he whispered and walked off toward the door. "We'll just get out of here so you can talk to Ben about his behaviour." George remarked to Ben's grandfather with mock respect. All of the boys excluding Ben and Nick made their way to the door.

George's gang convened on the front porch and George indicated they should be quiet. George leaned in to listen at the door in hopes of catching some of the **reprimand** he expected Ben to receive.

"Next time." They all heard the soft voice whisper. George startled as he saw a reflection in a window out of the corner of his eye. A shudder ran through his body as he turned just in time to see two glowing eyes fade from sight in the window pane.

CHAPTER TWELVE

The next morning Ben pulled his chair up silently to the breakfast table and sat twisting his napkin in his lap for a few moments. He knew it was wrong to have caused his grandparents so much worry and he spoke softly. "I'm sorry I worried you two last night. George challenged us to meet him there and I felt like I had a bit of an advantage since the Mason house doesn't scare me. I should have asked your permission before going out so late at night."

"Who knows what could have happened if your grandfather hadn't shown up. Those boys are well known for being trouble makers around here. You should just steer clear of them from now on." Gran scolded then changed the subject as she put a plate of toast and poached eggs down in front of Ben. "Did you call your father back when you got in last night?"

"I tried." Ben was relieved that she was going to let it go at that. "I thought it was weird that he didn't answer at ten thirty at night. Did he tell you he had somewhere to go last night?"

"No," Gran answered, "maybe he was already asleep by the time you called. Try him again tonight. What are your plans for today?"

"I want to get a start on a research project we were assigned yesterday and I'm probably getting together with Nick this afternoon. Do you need help with anything today?" Ben wondered why his grandparents hadn't assigned him any chores yet.

"I do need a few things from the Wilsons. Now that they have closed down their market in town I'll have to shop at their farm. Maybe you could go over there for me after you do your homework." Gran suggested.

"Sure, but why don't I go now and then I will do my homework after? I haven't thought of a topic yet; that will give me some time to think of an idea,"

"Thank you dear. Here is a list of what we need and here is some money." She handed him a piece of paper and a little leather pouch. "If you see anything you would like to buy, go ahead and add it on. I'll even cook it up for you if need be." She smiled warmly and patted him on the hand. "The Wilson's farm is just down the road from the Mason Manor. You can't miss it if you keep on that path.

Hard to believe that little path is all that is left of the road that used to be there. If we don't start using it once in a while it might grow right over."

This was good luck for Ben. He planned to stop in and see if he could get Alexa to appear. He walked across the yard and down the path enjoying the crispness in the air and the touch of colour that was beginning to show on the trees. He thought about the disappointment of the previous night and then decided that it was just as well that their plans were cut short. Any number of things could have gone wrong.

As he approached the house he noticed a movement on the front porch. He saw the faint image of a young girl reach up to an empty space and hold her arm up for a while and then lower it. She moved on and did the same in a new location. As he grew closer, Ben recognized Alexa even though her image a bit was faint and blurry. He realized that she was watering **fictitious** flowers. There must have been hanging baskets there at one time and it must have been her chore to care for them. He walked up to the porch, not knowing what to expect from this encounter with the spirit.

"Beautiful flowers. Are you too busy with your chores to talk right now?" he said.

"Hi Ben." Alexa's image became more solid in appearance as soon as she acknowledged him. "There are no flowers." She shook her head as if she just realized. "It was my job to care for the baskets. I guess it's just my routine to do what I did in my life. It's what I've been doing for so long now. What a thrill it would be to break that old routine." She laughed at herself and sat down on the steps with Ben.

"Things didn't go as we planned last night. I guess it wasn't meant to be. I think maybe it's better that you don't show yourself unnecessarily any way. Who knows what could happen." Ben realized the actuality of the statement only as he spoke it.

"I did get a little scare in though. I whispered to that mean boy and gave him quite a stare." Alexa smiled mischievously. "He caught a glimpse, but only just enough that he wasn't really sure if he saw anything. I think sometimes subtlety might be more effective than the sort of show you intended."

"You're right." Ben smiled with satisfaction. "So we accomplished what we planned and kept you safe. I guess everything worked out for the best then. I'm going to see Nick this afternoon. I'll see if I can talk him into coming here." Ben stood to leave. If Alexa was a real person, he might have touched her shoulder as he rose and he felt a little awkward not making the friendly gesture. He realized there would be a lot of ways that this friendship would require making adjustments.

"It would be lovely to see both of you. Goodbye then." Ben was amused at how Alexa's words sounded a little bit old fashion.

On the other side of the clearing of the manor house, Ben had to search a while to find the path that his grandmother had told him about. The brush and ivy had grown up quite a lot, but a couple of gravel ruts on the ground gave away the location of the path. He cleared away some of the **foliage** with his hands and stepped onto what was left of the old road. As he walked, Ben thought that he could hear an odd sound in the forest up ahead. He couldn't identify the noise. As he came closer to the sound he saw that what he had been hearing was small Bobcat tractor digging a hole in the ground. It struck Ben as a bit odd because of the fact that it was so far back in the bush.

Ben noticed a rickety shack tucked into the woods at the edge of the clearing. He stood beside it and watched the Bobcat dig. The little shack looked as if it had never been painted and moss grew all over the surface of the decaying wood. A part of the roof and one corner of the walls had caved in exposing the interior of the hovel. Ben lost interest in observing the construction and continued to skirt around the clearing; he followed the path that continued on the other side. The Bobcat operator was so intent on his work that he didn't see Ben.

A short time later Ben came to the back of a large red building. It was a barn, he realized and walked around to the front. He saw a middle aged woman in overalls arranging fruit and vegetables into large baskets in front of the barn. As he walked in her direction, Ben was distracted by a loud humming sound. He looked around for its source and realized that it came from a large fan on the side of a nearby building. The building was two stories high, but had no windows. It was covered in an unusual silver, metal siding that Ben had never seen before.

"Good morning." Ben shouted over the noise of the fan. "My grandmother sent me over to buy a few things. Are you Mrs.Wilson?"

"I am," she smiled warmly "and who would you be?"

"I'm Benjamin Rowan. I just moved in with my grandparents next door; Alice and Oscar Rowan. These raspberries look delicious." He commented picking up a basket of ripe fruit. "Gran won't mind if I add this to our order." Ben began to gather the items on his grandmother's list while he and Mrs. Wilson made small talk.

As Ben paid for his purchase, a man in ragged jeans and a plaid shirt walked over. "Where did you come from?" He questioned abruptly.

"I walked over from my grandparent's house." he answered. He picked up the brown bag that Mrs. Wilson had packed and scanned the bush looking for the path he had used. It was so grown over that Ben had difficulty finding the entrance to the path. The man took Ben by the shoulder, a little too firmly, and redirected him to a road nearby. It wasn't the same path Ben had come on, but he felt he was being encouraged to leave. He supposed he could easily find his way home this way anyhow.

Ben dropped the produce off to his grandmother, grabbed a ham sandwich for lunch and went upstairs to do some homework. He'd been thinking that it might be interesting to do his research project on ghosts. He might learn something that would be useful in relating to Alexa.

When he finished his homework he made another attempt to call his father. He was not surprised that there was no answer at this time of day so he left a message and headed off to Nick's house.

He walked up the pathway to Nick's house and noticed the distinct smell of **incense** burning and heard pan flute music coming from an open window. Ben knocked on the door and gazed at the little herb garden while he waited for an answer. Mrs. Follows soon came along and opened the door releasing a cloud of purple incense smoke and setting off the tinkling of numerous wind chimes.

"Hi Mrs. Follows." Ben smiled. "Is Nick home?"

"Come in dear." She welcomed Ben. "Nicholas, Ben is here for you." She bellowed as she showed him into the kitchen. She offered Ben a plate of lumpy green cookies, and since he couldn't think of a polite way to refuse, he accepted one. He took a bite and was dismayed to find that, with the exception of a small chocolate chip, it tasted more like a salad than a cookie.

Nick came bounding down the stairs, greeted Ben and snatched the cookie out of his hand. "Mom, don't subject my friends to your creations." he whined and threw the cookie into the garbage. "What do you feel like doing this afternoon, Ben?"

"I thought you might feel like going to explore in the manor house for a while." Ben tried not to sound too hopeful and was pleasantly surprised when Nick readily agreed.

"I need you to pick up some food for Rufus before you take off for the day, honey." Mrs. Follows remarked and handed Nick a twenty dollar bill. "He's out of dry food and he's sure to start in on the shoes again if we don't get him something to eat right away."

Nick and Ben went off to the pet supply store and on the way Ben told Nick about his visit with Alexa that morning. Nick gave Ben a high five when he heard that Alexa had managed to give George a fright the previous night.

"I went over to the Wilson's farm to get some stuff for Gran this morning." Ben commented. "I thought you said they were having money troubles."

"That's what everyone's saying. They shut down their produce stand and traded in their Honda Accord for an old van. Dad says they've been really keeping to themselves lately too. Why do you ask?"

"Nothing really; it was just that when I went there, I was surprised to see that they were getting ready to put up some sort of building way back in the bush. There was a Bobcat back there digging a hole for a foundation or something. You don't think they would open up a produce market on their own property do you? I'm a little worried about people getting that close to Mason Manor now that we have found out about Alexa."

"I can't see them building a produce stand way back in the bush. They'd put it on the road if anything; wouldn't they?" Nick said.

"Yeah, I guess they would, wouldn't they." Ben shrugged and **unconscientiously** put his hand over the key on his chest. "I just got worried cause I don't want anyone to scare Alexa back into hiding now that we've met her. It's pretty cool to be the only ones who know about her isn't it?"

"I'm still questioning if the whole thing really

happened. It's a lot to take in. I just went from not really believing in ghosts, to being friends with one." Nick shook his head and furrowed his brow. "Are you sure we didn't just dream up that whole incident?" Nick stopped outside a store front and waited for Ben's answer.

"I know it's hard to believe, but I've talked to her so many times now that there's no denying that she is real... If real is the word for it."

A **disheveled**, grey haired woman shuffled down the street towards the boys. As she walked she muttered to herself and pulled a ball of crumpled paper from her pocket. She smoothed out the wrinkles and, pointing to the top of the page began reciting the list out loud; though the boys could not make out what she was saying. She shuffled into the store and Ben noticed Nick shake his head and smile a little. "Who is that?" Ben asked.

"That is Miss Crumbey. She is the town cat lady. She lives on the far side of town and she has, probably twenty cats in that house with her. You can smell the place a block away and she is a nuisance to her neighbours, but she is pretty harmless."

They stepped into the store and Nick began looking for the right brand of dog food for Rufus. Miss Crumbey puttered around beside the boys studying the labels on various packages before deciding on a large bag. The old woman struggled to lift the bag and fell backward as it slipped loose from the shelf. She landed on her behind on the wooden floor and the thirty pound bag of food landed, with a distinct crunching sound, on top of her, pinning her to the floor. Only her legs, with sagging stockings and red sneakers, protruded from beneath the bag.

Seeing the small woman's struggle, the two boys immediately stepped forward, each taking an end of the bag, and lifted the weight from the **pugnacious** woman. She stood, gave the bag a firm kick and muttered at it in anger.

"This is probably the wrong food, isn't it Miss Crumbey?" Nick said softly. "This is dog food. You were probably looking for cat food." Nick moved to put the bag back in place on the shelf and said, "The cat food is over on the next isle. Do you want me to show you?"

"No." The woman grumbled, reading the label on the bag, then rechecking her list. "I know what I'm looking for. Would you kindly bring that up to the front counter for me?" she demanded.

Nick carried the dog food up to the front counter and returned to look for Rufus's food. "That's weird." He commented to Ben. "I wonder if she has started to take in dogs too. That ought to make her neighbours happy; all those cats and dogs in the same house.

CHAPTER THIRTEEN

After returning the bag of dog food to the Follows house, the two boys walked over to Mason Manor. Ben walked up the front stairs with Nick close behind. Ben knocked and reached for the door knob, when Nick grabbed his hand before he could open it. "Let me knock too, before you open the door." he rushed to say. "I guess I'm being a bit superstitious, but I'd just feel better."

Nick reached over to knock, but before he did both boys heard the sound of running footsteps inside the house. They turned toward each other, wide eyed. "I don't think that's Alexa!" Ben quickly bent to peer through the key hole. "Someone is in there."

"How do you know it's not Alexa? She could be in there running around. Maybe ghosts need exercise too." Nick said.

"Come on Nick. This is serious. Who could be in there? We have to find out who it is. What if Alexa doesn't realize and she appears when that person can see her?"

"Let's have a peek." Nick walked to the window that looked into the foyer. "I can't see anyone." He whispered. "Let's go in."

Ben reached for the door knob again and Nick stopped him a second time. "Do we need to knock again?" He looked tense which made Ben's fear feel more real.

"No." He opened the door and peered in. "We already knocked; besides you don't need to get so hung up on it. It's just common courtesy."

The boys slipped in the door, quickly scanned the foyer and tiptoed into the next room. They found that they were in what had once been the dining room. They saw no one and were about to leave when Nick nudged Ben and pointed at the floor. There were distinct foot prints in the dust on the floor. Someone had apparently walked into the room and turned around and left.

"Someone is looking for something." Ben whispered. "They must be making trouble or they wouldn't have hidden when they heard us."

Nick peeked out into the foyer and tiptoed out of the room again. They crossed the foyer and were about to go into another room when they heard a floor board creek upstairs. "Alexa." Ben whispered. "Where are you? Who is here? Can you tell me?" He waited a moment and when there was no response he indicated to Nick that they should go upstairs. They peered up to the loft above and, seeing no one they began to climb the stairs. When they reached the top they stopped to listen for signs of the intruder.

"He's in danger Ben." They heard Alexa whisper. "Get him out of here." The voice sounded haunting even to Ben. When he turned to Nick he could see that even though Nick should not be afraid of Alexa, his face had gone pale at the sound of her disembodied voice.

"Who is here Alexa?" Ben questioned, but before there was time for a response, they heard a loud creaking sound followed by a crash and a yelp. Ben and Nick ran in the direction of the sound. They reached a door at the end of the hall way and tried to open it. It was stuck. They looked around, but realized that this was the only place that the sound could have come from.

"Are you okay?" Ben yelled through the door. They heard a scuffling sound. "Who is in there?" Ben yelled. When there was no answer Ben tried the door again. He lodged his shoulder into the door, but it didn't give. "Is there someone in there?" He said.

There was the sound of wood cracking and then a boy's voice called "Help me!"

Both Ben and Nick looked to each other. Recognizing that the voice belonged to a kid, they knew they had to help. They moved back from the door; Nick gave a count of three and the boys both lunged at the door together. It creaked as they strained their weight against it and then it fell open. The boys stumbled over the threshold and scrambled to gain their footing. They could see very little in the shadowy stairwell, but they were able to make out a broken railing at the top of the stairs. Ben crept forward and looked over the edge beside the dangling piece of wood. From there he could see a hand that clung tightly to the other end of the fallen railing. Ben reached out and grasped the hand around the wrist. He pulled, but it became obvious that the weight of the other person was more than he could handle on his own. "Nick, help me." Ben urged, and his friend moved forward, grabbed the wrist as well and both boys pulled.

"Wait!" shouted the boy on the stairwell. "I'm stuck. Let me get my foot out of this hole and I'll tell you when to pull." They heard a rustling sound from below and the boy yelped in pain. They felt his arm tugging against the pressure they applied. "I can't get loose." He whimpered. "Help me. Please."

"I'll go down and see if I can find the bottom of the stairs." Ben called down to him. "Nick, you stay here and hold onto him. If I can find the bottom of the stairs, I'll climb up and try to get his foot loose. You hang in there buddy." He shouted down the stairwell. "I'll be right there."

Ben raced from the room, ran down the hall and turned sharply at the stairs that led down to the foyer. He grabbed the railing and began, very quickly, to descend the stairs when his foot slipped out from under him. His heels thumped down three or four stairs and he lost his grip on the railing. He felt himself gaining momentum as he bumped feet first down the stairs and scrambled to right himself. Just as Ben felt he was going to tumble head first to the bottom of the stairs, he felt an icy grip on his arm and a second chilling hand on his chest. He came to a stop, found his footing and righted himself. Out of breath and tingling with **adrenaline** he paused to get his bearing. "Thank you." He whispered and resumed his descent to the bottom.

Ben guessed at the approximate location of the other end of the stairwell and ran in that direction. He opened one door and found it led into a room. The next door he tried was stuck. He threw his shoulder against the door and it didn't open. From inside he heard a frantic voice call, "I can't hold on. I'm slipping!"

Ben rammed his shoulder into the door again and grunted in pain and dismay at the frustration of his failed attempt. He looked around in hopes of finding something to assist his efforts. Ben became conscious of the key's coldness on his chest and he heard the words *"try again"* inside his head. He rubbed his aching shoulder, took a deep breath and slammed his body against the door for a third time. It popped open. Ben strained his eyes in the darkness. He could see the bottom of the stairwell and he felt around for a hand railing. When he found it he placed a tentative foot on the bottom step. The wood felt spongy under his weight and he felt around for a firmer foothold. The second step felt more solid, but as he climbed, he tested each stair with his foot before trusting it with his full weight. This slowed his progress, but he knew it was necessary if he was going to make it to the boy at the top.

When Ben estimated that he must be near the top of the stairs he spoke softly. "Are you there?" He didn't know if he was asking for Alexa or the captive of the stairwell.

"I can't hold on much longer. Can you see what my foot is stuck on?" said the anxious voice.

"I can't see anything." Ben replied. "I'm going to feel around a bit." Ben felt the surface of one step, but found nothing. He moved up a step and found that space vacant too. As he moved his foot up so that he could feel around on the next step, he realized, too late, that the wood was rotten. His foot broke through the surface and his leg plunged into emptiness. He grabbed the stair rail and tried to support his weight with his arms. He pulled himself up with his arms and with the foot that was free. He had to wiggle his foot to get it loose and placed it on the more stable stair below.

"Are you okay Ben!" Nick called urgently.

"I fine. I'm just looking for this guy's foot, but I can't see a thing. Let me see if I can reach the next step. I can't get up any farther. The next step is rotten." Ben strained to reach the next stair and finally found the leg of the intruder, with the foot wedged into the crumbling wood. He pulled up on the boy's leg and stopped when he heard him cry out in pain.

"Don't stop. Even if it hurts me, you're going to just have to pull my leg out; otherwise I'm going to fall."

Ben grabbed the cuff of the boy's pant leg and pulled up at the same time as he tore away bit of the rotten wood with his other hand. After a few minutes the hole had grown large enough and with careful guidance, Ben twisted the boy's foot and it came loose from the board. The boy exclaimed in pain and relief and called "I'm loose. Nick, can you lower me and Ben, check where there is a solid step for me to get down to."

"You know who we are?" Nick questioned in surprise as he lowered the boy's weight from above.

Ben guided the boy's foot to the step that he had just been standing on. "Can you walk on that leg?" he said into the darkness.

"No," said the mystery person, "but I can sit on the stairs and slide myself down."

109

"Just be careful. A lot of the stairs are rotten. Come slowly and support yourself on the railing. Nick, meet us downstairs." Ben called up.

As Ben slowly made his way to the bottom of the stairs, he heard Nick's footsteps running up the hallway. He reached for the injured boy and supported him under the arm. The two boys moved into the light and Ben saw Nick's expression transform in surprise. "Jason?" he questioned. "What are you doing here?"

Ben noticed the boy's jeans and black t-shirt and knew he was one of George's gang. He too, wondered what the boy was doing at Mason Manor. "Are you okay? Your ankle is bleeding."

"It does hurt." He said, bending to examine his injury. He rubbed his ankle **gingerly** and looked at Nick. "Don't say that I told you, but George sent me. He wanted me to look around. He figured you had set something up to trick him. He said I should look around the first floor for something that you might have put there to try to scare us the other night."

"We didn't set anything up. Did something scare George?" Nick asked. "Sit down, Jason I think your ankle is pretty bad."

"I don't know what George saw. He didn't want to come here himself. To tell the truth, I didn't want to come here either, but I was more scared of George than whatever it was that he saw here." Jason admitted. "I think he was just scared cause of all the ghost stories."

"Did you see anything?" Ben asked. "We heard some scary sounds after you guys left, but we didn't stick around to find out what it was because my grandfather was with us."

"The only thing I saw that was scary today was those stairs. Man, this place is old and rickety. I don't know if I can walk home." he mumbled to himself.

"We can help you get home if you like." Ben offered.

"Thanks." Jason accepted. Ben and Nick each took a side and offered Jason support for the walk home. "Do you mind taking the long way? I don't want George to see me getting help from you guys. No **offence**, but he'll give me a real hard time."

"No offence taken, buddy." Nick said. "I don't like being on George's bad side. No point in you being there too. I hope we can maybe be friends from now on; if we keep it quiet. What do you think?"

"Are you kidding me?" Jason's voice piped. "You guys really saved my butt here today. I owe you guys. If we can keep it on the sly, I'd be glad to be friends."

CHAPTER FOURTEEN

Ben and Nick returned to the manor house after escorting Jason home. Jason's ankle was bleeding pretty badly and his mother had taken him to the doctor to have it checked out. The boys had agreed that they wouldn't talk openly at school, but that they would quietly be friendly.

Nick walked up the porch steps first and knocked on the front door. Ben followed him through the door and called out to Alexa. There was no answer and the boys looked around the room expectantly. Ben looked at Nick and watched as his eyes widened in surprise. Ben looked in the direction that Nick was staring and he saw a figure in a wall tapestry which seemed to become three dimensional and then slowly immerge from the picture.

"Hello." Alexa smiled. "How is the boy who fell on the stairs?"

"He'll be fine and I don't think you'll see him around here again. He was afraid to come here today, but he was too afraid of George to say no." Ben walked to the stair case in the foyer and placed a foot on the bottom step. "Do you mind if Nick and I look around the house a little? We just came here to see you and explore a bit."

When Alexa didn't answer, Ben turned around to where he expected her to be. She was not there. "Alexa is gone." he said to Nick. "Did you see her disappear?"

Nick shook his head and the boys looked around the room for her. Ben called out to her then motioned for Nick to follow him up the stairs. They went up stairs and began to walk along the hallway. They went into the first room on the hall and found it to be empty. They left the room in search of a room that would be more interesting. A few doors down the hall Ben came to another room. He reached for the door knob and was surprised at the coldness he felt on the knob. He grasped the knob and turned, but found the door to be locked.

He was about to move on to the next room when he heard a sound from within the locked room. He motioned to Nick and leaned close to the door to listen. At first he wasn't sure what he was hearing and then, as he and Nick listened longer, it became apparent that it was the sound of someone softly crying. He called out gently to Alexa and waited. The crying continued. Ben pulled the key from his shirt and found it to be warm from his body heat. He bent over and tried it in the door lock. It fit, but when he tried to turn the key, it wouldn't move. Ben called out to Alexa again, his concern evident in his voice.

"I'm here." He heard a voice say, simply, from down the hall. The boys looked at each other, then at the door; the crying had stopped. They walked in the direction Alexa's voice had come from.

They came to a room at the end of the hall and entered it. The room was cold and Ben felt a shiver run up his spine as he entered. The walls were lined with shelves from floor to ceiling and many of the shelves still contained books. Some books had fallen from shelves and lay in piles upon the floor. The room had the musty smell of decaying paper and dust. A couple of leather couches sat in the middle of the room, facing each other. Alexa sat on one of the couches looking intently down at her hands as if she was reading a book. Though there was no book in her hands, she reached up with a finger, touched it to her tongue and reached back to her lap and flicked her finger in mid air as if to turn a page. Ben saw Nick shudder and take a step backwards. Ben walked into the room, sat down across from Alexa and leaned back into the couch.

"What are you reading?"

Ben watched as Alexa looked up from her book, focused on him, placed a nonexistent marker in the book and moved as if closing the cover. As she moved through these actions her image became more clear, until the girl sitting before him looked as real as the boy who lingered timidly beside the entrance to the room. "It is a play by William Shakespeare. Though, now that you speak to me, I can see that there was no book at all. I read the same book every day. I long to read any other of these books, but every day it is the only book I can pick up. It would be so nice to break these old routines."

"We heard someone crying down the hall. I thought it was you, but you're sitting here so peacefully; I can't imagine you were just crying were you?"

"That's my mother. I hear her crying and calling my name sometimes, but when I go to where I hear her voice, there is no one there. I wish so dearly to see my mother, but it is only the sound of her voice. It is only in my bedroom that she cries and calls my name. It's really quite eerie sometimes."

Ben smiled at the irony of a ghost finding another ghost eerie. "You don't know why she is crying?"

"I suppose she is missing me. It's like she's lost me, even though I'm right here." Alexa shook her head.

"I've been reading about spirits lately; for a school project. I read that sometimes, when something really **traumatic** happens somewhere, when someone has really strong emotions, their image can be imprinted on a place. It's not really a ghost, it's more like a picture that's been taken that plays over and over again. Maybe that's what it is. Maybe that's why you can't see your mother, or talk to her." Alexa nodded thoughtfully and Ben continued, eager to ask the questions he had come here to ask.

"Why are you here, Alexa?" Ben blurted out. "I've been reading that ghosts have unfinished business. They have something that they need to find closure about and that's why their spirit doesn't move on to the afterlife. What's your unfinished business? Do you need help with something?"

"I don't know, Ben." She thought for a few moments. "I can't remember. I know that there is something I am searching for. I walk around this house looking and looking and I can't remember what it is that I am looking for. I think I used to know, but I've been doing the same thing every day for so long now that I have forgotten what it is that I need to find."

"That must be frustrating." Nick finally stepped forward. "Maybe if Ben and I help, you can figure it out."

"I suppose a fresh **perspective** would help." Alexa looked hopeful. "It would also be helpful to have someone searching, who can actually move things. I can only look at the surface of things. I can't open doors or pick things up. It's really quite **exasperating**."

"But wasn't that you, earlier, who helped me open the door?" Ben puzzled

"You know, I hadn't thought of it." Alexa wrinkled her brow. "I did help open that door. In the urgency of the moment, I just did it. Do you think that I am capable of moving things?" She spoke more quickly as the possibilities dawned on her. "If I can move things; that means that I could read a different book. I could pick up things I have wanted to hold. I could search this house for whatever it is that is keeping me here!"

"Here," Nick reached into his pocket, "try to move this." He pulled out a Smartie and placed it on the heavy wooden table between the two couches. "Start with something small. See if you can push this off the table."

Alexa reached out, extended her finger and moved toward the little yellow chocolate. Her finger slowly neared the object and as she continued to move, her finger went through the Smartie and then through the table until her hand disappeared into the surface. She looked at what appeared to be the stump of her wrist with frustration, shook her head and frowned as she withdrew her hand. "That is what always happens. My hand goes right through things. The only things I can pick up are things that are not actually there. **Figments** of my memory, like that book I thought I was reading."

"That's not exactly true." Ben shook his head. "I distinctly felt you touch me when you stopped me from falling down the stairs earlier. You grabbed my right arm and put your hand on my chest. You didn't exactly move me; you kept me from falling. That's the same thing right?"

"Maybe it's because you're alive. Try touching Ben now." Nick nodded in Ben's direction.

Alexa reached out toward Ben's hand which was resting on his knee. Her hand sunk through Ben's and into his knee. Ben shuddered and Alexa quickly removed her hand.

"How did you feel when you thought I was going to fall down the stairs?" Ben asked Alexa. "Maybe it has something to do with feeling a strong emotion."

"I did feel afraid for you, but that doesn't explain how I helped open doors does it? You two go ahead and look around some more. I'm going to stay here and work on this a while. I'll try moving this little yellow thing and I'll think about what it might be that I'm always searching for."

CHAPTER FIFTEEN

The boys looked around the house for a while and then tried to get Alexa to appear again. When they were unsuccessful at **conjuring** their ghostly friend, they decided to go home. Ben walked Nick to his house and as they came up the sidewalk, nearing his house, they heard Mrs. Follows calling out for Rufus over and over.

"Hey Mom. Did Rufus take off on you?"

"I put him in the back yard earlier today." Mrs. Follows wrung her hands together. "At about two o'clock I heard him barking and growling a lot. I assumed that that grey cat was sitting on the fence again, tormenting him and I just yelled out for him to be quiet. He seemed to calm down after that, so I didn't think about him again until a few minutes ago when I went to give him his food. He was gone. I don't know how he got out of the back yard. The gate was still latched. Do you think he could have jumped the fence?"

"I guess he must have. Ben and I will go looking for him. Don't worry Mom."

The boys continued down the street calling out for Rufus. They looked in alleyways and backyards. They searched the park and the river bank. They searched places a dog would like to go. They went to the garbage site, the butcher shop, the fish monger, the pet food store and the field behind the abandoned warehouse. There was no sign of Rufus.

"I hate to bring it up, Nick, but have you thought about all the missing dogs there've been lately? What if George and his gang grabbed Rufus to try to get back at us? Maybe we should go to that place where they were hanging around in the bush the other day."

"I've been trying not to think about that, but you're right. Rufus couldn't have jumped that fence. Someone took him out of there. Let's go check out the spot where we saw those guys."

The boys hurried across town and were nearing the path to the gang's gathering place. As they got closer to their destination a thought occurred to Nick. "We should snoop around at Miss Crumbey's house a bit too. It could be her taking the dogs. Why else would she be buying dog food?"

Ben agreed and the boys stopped at the crosswalk

across the street from Miss. Crumbey's house. A van pulled up and stopped at the stop sign. Ben recognized the man from the Wilson farm and saw him give a friendly wave to Nick. Nick returned his wave and the boys continued across the street in front of the van. "He was a lot friendlier to you than he was to me the other day." Ben said.

Nick opened his mouth to respond, but stopped when the boys heard a dog barking. "That sounds like Rufus!" Nick started to run. "Let's go!"

He ran across the street with Ben close on his heels and the two boys darted behind a shrub near the house. Nick ran up to the side of the house and pressed himself against the wall. Ben joined him and the two boys crept along the wall until they came to a window. Nick stood on his toes to attempt to look into the window, but it was too high. Ben hunched down on the ground under the window and braced himself on his hands and knees. Nick tentatively stepped up onto Ben's back and grabbed the window sill. He pulled himself up slowly and peered into the window. He was startled by a sudden movement close to where he stood and ducked down, afraid of being discovered. With his heart pounding he peeked over the window sill again and realized that the movement had been a cat jumping down from the window ledge inside the house. Nick looked further into the room and saw that Miss Crumbey was bending over in front of a large plastic crate; the kind people transport dogs in. She pushed a bowl into the crate as she held something back inside it with her other hand. She quickly withdrew her hand and closed the gate on the front of the crate. Miss Crumbey shuffled from the room and four cats quickly convened on top of the crate. Just then Ben's arms collapsed from Nick's weight and Nick tumbled to the ground in front of him.

Nick laid flat on his stomach on the ground beside the front porch of the house and Ben was surprised to hear him whisper as he looked into the space under the floor of the porch. "What are you doing in there?" He picked himself up off the ground and squatted facing an opening under the porch.

"I'm just keeping a low *profile*." Ben was surprised to hear a girl's voice from within the dark space. "What are you two up to?" A face appeared from between the boards. It was a girl that Ben estimated was about the same age as he and Nick. Her face, although smudged with dirt, wore a friendly expression. She wiggled out from under the porch and reached back from where she had just come and extracted a book and a flashlight. Her blond hair was pulled back into a messy ponytail and a cobweb and a stick clung to a clump of hair that had fallen loose from the elastic.

"We're looking for my dog." Nick answered. "Have you heard any dogs barking while you were under there?"

"I heard one just a minute ago, but that was it. Why

would you be looking for your dog at Miss Crumbey's house? You put a dog in there with all those cats and you'd have quite a nasty pot of soup." The girl's pretty face contorted into a bizarre sneer briefly, then she turned to Ben and said, "Who are you? I've never seen you around here before."

"This is my friend, Ben." Nick rushed to answer. "He just moved here, but you should have seen him at school last week."

"Why do you think I'm hiding under here?" She turned to Nick with an exaggerated facial expression of questioning. "I didn't go to school last week and I'm pretty sure they're looking for me. They work from nine to five, so I figure if I have good enough hiding places during their work hours, I can go home after supper time and, I estimate it should be at least another week before they catch up with me. I'm Ricky." she held out her hand to greet Ben and gave a very firm shake when he extended his own hand.

"We're going to keep looking for Rufus. There's a spot we want to check out in the bush up the street from here." Nick attempted to end the conversation with Ricky.

"Be careful going up there. George and his gang have been hanging around up there. You don't want him to think you're spying on them." Ricky warned. "They're building something up there. I don't know what it is yet, but I just saw Tommy heading up there with a big cardboard box." She shrugged her shoulders, tucked her book and flashlight into her backpack and slung it over her arm. "I'll come with you guys. I know a good spot where you can look into the clearing without being seen."

Nick flashed a look of dismay to Ben and the three snuck out of Miss Crumbey's yard. Ricky looked from side to side as they neared the street and suddenly sprinted up the street to the path in the woods. Nick whispered "She's kinda weird. No one hangs around with her." and the two boys followed her up the path.

When they were coming close to the clearing, Ricky veered off the path and motioned for the boys to follow her. They climbed over a log, wrestled through a thick patch of brush and struggled up a hill slippery with wet leaves. At the top of the hill they were able to peek over and see the clearing that George's gang had been **frequenting** lately. Five boys were huddled together over something that was not visible from the hill top. The three children watched and strained to see what had the gang's interest. Eventually one of the gang boys stood up and moved from the group to retrieve something from his backpack. At that moment the children could briefly see that what they were gathered around was black in colour.

Nick suddenly stood up and yelled "They have Rufus!" and he charged down the hill at the group of boys. Caught off guard by Nick's sudden outburst, Ben followed a few moments later and Ricky cautiously tailed behind. The boys in the clearing scrambled to hide a number of objects and as they moved the black item it became obvious that it was fabric, not fur. Nick stopped short and attempted to turn back the way he had come, but slipped and fell into a mud puddle.

"You again!" The gang leader jumped to his feet and clenched his fists. "What are you doing following us around? I'm getting tired of you two always getting in our way. We're going to have to teach you a lesson. Kevin and Mark, you grab that one." George said, indicating Nick. "Tommy and me will take care of the new kid"

Kevin and Mark rushed forward towards Nick. Mark stopped short of the puddle and reached out to grab Nick, but his feet slid in the slippery mud and he fell, face first into the puddle. Kevin was following closely behind and did not stop soon enough. His feet also made contact with the slippery mud. As his first foot slipped out from under him, he scrambled to brace himself with his other foot. It also slipped out from under him and he alternated trying to gain his footing on one foot then the other until he fell into the puddle as well, on top of Mark.

In the meantime, George and Tommy went after Ben. Ben was tempted to run, but didn't want to abandon his friend who was stuck in the mud. Ben dodged as George lunged at him and avoided being caught. Ben jumped aside to avoid George's next attempt to grab him, but in his rush to **evade** George, landed right in Tommy's grasp. Tommy gripped Bens arm and twisted it sharply behind his back. Tommy held Ben by the twisted arm and seized him by the throat with the other arm. Ben was briefly distracted by the feeling of the key tingling against his chest and then George stepped forward, sneering and punched Ben in the stomach. Ben reacted automatically by doubling over in pain and coughing. His bending had jarred him loose from Tommy's grip, but Tommy reacted by kicking Ben in the backside hard enough to knock him forward. As Ben lurched head first to the ground, he was alarmed to see the key sailing away from him and skidding across the grass. George made an attempt to kick Ben, but Ben scrambled out of the way. As he jumped back to his feet, he caught a glimpse of Ricky's blond hair, but on taking a second look, she was nowhere to be seen.

Tommy, once again, crept up behind Ben and grasped both of his arms and twisted them painfully behind Ben's back. George smirked and advanced toward Ben. George swung his fist at Ben and made contact with his jaw. Ben felt the surge of pain swell through his face and saw stars in his eyes. When his vision began to clear he saw that George was shaking his hand as if to shake off the pain of the punch. George saw that Ben was watching him and stepped forward again; his anger renewed by his own show of weakness. Just before he was about to swing again, a loud cracking sound came from behind George. George turned toward the sound and screamed in fright to see a tall tree leaning from the forest over his head. He seemed to be frozen in fear and then the tree began to tilt more and more in his direction. An especially loud cracking sound jarred him from his trance and just before the tree came crashing down he jumped out of the way and ran from the clearing.

There was a sudden flurry of activity as the gang boys scrambled to gather up their belongings and follow George from the forest.

Ben stood in the same spot for quite some time, dazed by the situation. He shook his head and turned to look for Nick. He spotted Nick, still sitting in the mud puddle looking blindly at the fallen tree. Ben walked over and offered his hand to his friend and pulled him up from the puddle.

"Where's Ricky." Nick said.

This question drew Ben to awareness and his arm jerked up to his chest where the key usually rested. He felt around for it under his shirt and then rushed to the area where he had seen it fall in the grass. "The key, Nick! It fell off! Help me find it!" Ben dropped to his hands and knees and began to pat the ground all around him.

Nick rushed forward to assist his friend and as the two searched the grass, Ricky stepped forward from the forest. "Is this what you're looking for?" She held up the key still attached to the leather tie.

"Yes!" Ben jumped up and snatched it from her

hand. He strung the cord around his neck, carefully tucked the key inside his shirt and placed his hand protectively over the key on his chest. He took a few deep breaths and continued to clutch the key, but seemed to come to his senses after a moment. "I'm sorry, Ricky. That was rude of me. Thanks for keeping my key safe. Are you okay?"

"Yeah, I'm okay, but what just happened? Can you believe those guys? Where do they get off?" She looked more and more outraged as she continued to speak.

"What I'd like to know is; how did that tree happen to fall just when we needed it to?" Nick said.

"That was kind of strange." Ricky said. "I was trying to push it over the whole time those guys were after you two; just to distract them. I wasn't getting anywhere with it, but I saw you drop that key. I snuck out and picked up the key, then I went back to try to push the tree over again. It was like I suddenly had super powers. I had, like, the strength of ten men. I gave that tree one push and it fell over." Ricky's face was flushed with her victory over the gang boys and the tree.

Ben gave Nick a knowing look and patted Ricky on the shoulder. "That was great. Thanks a lot for your help. You could have just run away. You're a good friend."

Ricky's face broke into a wide grin and she nodded her head to the side. "Any time Ben. I got your back." She raised her hand up in front of her eyes and rubbed her palm with her thumb. "By the way, what is that key made of, anyway? It was so cold when I picked it up that it left a mark on my hand."

CHAPTER SIXTEEN

The next few weeks passed uneventfully. Ben was still very sad about the loss of his mother, but he no longer felt completely **immobilized** by the sorrow. He was confused by the distance he felt growing between himself and his father. For a while Ben had felt closer than ever to his father. Their shared grief seemed to unite them. Lately though, his father phoned less often and when they did talk, his dad always seemed **preoccupied** and aloof.

The leaves were in full colour, the school year was progressing as expected and Ben and Nick's friendship grew. The boys often found themselves in the company of Ricky. At first they tolerated her presence because of her help during the incident in the forest; eventually they grew to like her in spite of her odd ways. She joined them for lunch break at school and walked with them on the way home, but the boys didn't share the secret of Alexa with her. Though she lived closer to the school, Ben often saw Ricky when he went to the Wilson's farm to pick up produce for his grandmother.

Ben was on his way to the Wilson's after stopping at Mason Manor. He had been unsuccessful at coxing Alexa out for a visit and he continued on to the farm feeling disappointed. Ben continued to take the short cut through the forest when going to the Wilson's, but was more careful not to let Mr. Wilson see him emerge from the forest path. He hid behind the **decrepit** shack and watched the fast progress of the building project in the clearing. He was still curious about why Mr. Wilson would need a building so far removed from the farm.

Ben came to the wooded area just behind the Wilson's barn. He skirted around back of the barn and peeked around the corner to be sure he wouldn't get caught coming from the forest. Ben came out of the forest on the road which was the normal entrance to the farm and continued back to the barn where Mrs. Wilson usually kept her produce artfully displayed. As he walked up, Ben could see that Ricky was helping Mrs. Wilson to place produce into large wicker baskets in front of the red building. The woman and the girl were pleasantly engaged in casual conversation and didn't notice his arrival at first.

"Your parents allow you to stay out that late, do they?" Mrs. Wilson gave Ricky a look of concern.

"Oh yeah; they don't care. I can do whatever I want

most of the time. My mom tells me I shouldn't go swimming alone, but I can do pretty much anything else. My mom and dad are never around anyway. I'm pretty independent." Ricky rubbed her hands together to remove any dirt and folded her arms across her chest.

Mrs. Wilson shook her head, sighed deeply and continued on with her chore. Ben stepped forward and said, "Hi Ricky, hi Mrs. Wilson. Really nice display you've made. Gran sent me over to pick up some squash for a casserole she is making for dinner. She said acorn or butternut would both work, but I don't know which is which. Could you show me please?"

Mrs. Wilson smiled, stopped what she was doing and selected two different gourds for Ben to choose from. He shrugged and chose the dark green one with the zigzag sides. He picked up some carrots, potatoes and onions and paid Mrs. Wilson. As she arranged his purchase in a paper bag, Ben turned to Ricky to chat. "You working here all day?"

"Just a bit longer. I'll come find you later when I'm done here. What are you and Nick up to today?"

"We're going to the library to look up some information for the socials homework and then we're just going to hang around. If you don't find us at the library or Nick's house, check the park on Bridal Avenue."

Ben said goodbye and walked back up the road again.

He knew he was still too early to go to Nick's house yet so he doubled back down the forest path to look for Alexa again. He could see her faint image on the front porch watering the flower baskets and quickened his step so that she would see him before she finished her job and disappeared again. He called out to her when he was close enough and, as usual, her image appeared to become more solid as she turned to greet him.

The two sat on the steps together and chatted like old friends. "Are you making any progress with moving things?" Ben asked.

"No; it's so frustrating. I know I can do it, but only under special circumstances. If only I could figure out what it takes to make it happen." Alexa smoothed down her skirt with her hands impatiently. "I think our search of the house would be much faster if I were helping you and Nick. How about your mystery? Have you made any progress in figuring out who is taking the dogs?"

"No we haven't, and Nick is so worried about Rufus. It's been over three weeks since he went missing. We've been trying to listen in on conversations that the gang boys are having, but they are too suspicious of us. We can't get close enough to hear what they're saying."

"Maybe I can help with that!" Alexa face brightened. "If there were a way you could get the key close to them, I'm sure I could listen in on them and tell you what I hear!" Her face took on a serious expression, "We just have to be careful to keep the key safe."

"That's a great idea." Ben nodded hopefully. "Let me think on a way to do that. I'll let you know what I come up with. Nick and I will come back later this afternoon to search the house with you. We pretty much finished looking through everything in the den. Which room do you want to do next?"

Before Ben had even finished his last sentence, Alexa unexpectedly disappeared. She had never done this before and Ben stared at the place she had been sitting, feeling dumbfounded. He stared in silence for a moment when his thoughts were interrupted.

"Ben! Over here, Ben!" He heard Ricky's voice from across the field. "You forgot your bag of vegetables at the barn! I was just bringing it to your grandma's house." Her volume decreased as she grew closer, and she set the paper bag down on the top step before plunking down on the stairs beside him. "Who was that girl you were talking to? I've never seen her around here before."

Ben was caught off guard by the question. It had just dawned on him, why Alexa had disappeared so suddenly and had yet to occur to him that Ricky might have seen her as she had approached. "I – Unh – Who..." Ben stuttered. "That girl, oh, unh, she..." He struggled to come up with an answer that would cover for Alexa, yet not force him to lie to Ricky.

Both children startled as they heard a crunching sound and the paper bag of vegetables seemed to fly off of the stairs and tumble to the ground. Carrots, potatoes and onions spilled out on the moss all around the path and the acorn squash split in half as it hit the stone walk way.

Ricky's mouth was agape as she stared at the vegetable strewn path. Ben had to make a concerted effort to suppress his smile. It was clear to him what had just occurred as he felt the coolness of the key against his skin. Alexa had caused a distraction to buy him time to come up with an answer for Ricky. He was also thrilled to realize that Alexa had been able to use the skill that had eluded her for weeks. She had moved an object!

"That squash must have shifted and knocked the bag down. I hope Gran doesn't mind a broken squash." Ben laughed and he began to gather up the spilled vegetables. "That girl said she lives nearby, but she doesn't go to our school. We only talked for a bit before she had to get going. Can you walk back to my house with me, or do you have to go back to the Wilson's?" Ben changed the subject quickly.

"Mrs. Wilson said it was up to me if I come back or not. She was going to get me some lunch, but I'm not that hungry." Ricky said, reluctantly choosing friendship over a meal. "She's always trying to feed me. She doesn't realize that I'm pretty good at **fending** for myself."

"My Gran will get us some lunch." Ben smiled. "I guess women just like to feed people."

Ben and Ricky finished the sandwiches that Gran had made. Ben was astounded that Ricky ate twice as much as he did. Gran cleared away their plates and put a tray of homemade cookies down in front of them. Ben felt certain that Ricky would be too full to eat cookies, but she dug in and ate three. Ben ate one and put three into his jacket pocket.

Ben and Ricky headed over to Nick's house. Nick was sitting outside on the front step when they arrived. He sat with his elbow resting on his knees and his chin in his hand.

"You're missing Rufus, aren't you?" Ben asked and reached into his pocket. He handed Nick the three cookies he had stashed away earlier and sat down beside his friend.

"These are awesome!" Nick sputtered through the crumbs. "You're so lucky your Gran is a good cook. My mom made veggie burgers for lunch today, but if it was hockey season, I might have wondered if some team out there was missing their puck."

"I'd be happy with the puck burger if I was you. My mother doesn't cook. Half the time she doesn't even bring home any groceries. This morning I was going to make a peanut butter sandwich, but there was no bread, so I just had peanut butter for breakfast." Ricky looked embarrassed and tried to make light of what she had just said. "I'm surprised that my tongue isn't still glued to the roof of my mouth."

"Your parents don't really take care of you, do they?" Ben spoke gently, not wanting Ricky to take offence.

"I guess you could say that." Ricky said. "It can have its advantages though; like no curfew, no rules, no getting grounded. I've got it made when you think about it." She looked awkward and changed the topic quickly. "Should we get over to the library?"

On the way to the library Ben stopped to read a paper taped to the side of a mailbox. "Look guys," he motioned toward the poster, "another missing dog. This one is a Pitt Bull Terrier. It's been missing for two days now."He looked thoughtful for a moment. "What is that now? Five or six missing dogs, isn't it?"

"That's six including Rufus. We need to find out what is going on here. I want my dog back. What should we do next?" Nick said.

Ben hesitated then said, "Alexa had an idea, but I need to think it through." He wondered again if they should bring Ricky in on their secret. It was becoming difficult to keep the secret from her when she was with them so often.

"Who's Alexa?" Ricky looked away abruptly and interrupted her own question."Look at that!" She nodded toward the skate park that was across the parking lot from the library. George and some of his friends were there and George was showing them a large white bandage on his right forearm. "I wonder what happened to him."

Ben noticed that Jason was one of the boys admiring the injury. He hopped they might have an opportunity to speak to him alone later.

An hour later the three children walked out of the library each holding a few books. Ben was excited to see Jason sitting alone at the bus stop beside the skate park. He looked around for any of the other gang boys and was pleased to see that this would be a good opportunity to talk to Jason. He made the suggestion to his companions and the three children crossed the street and greeted Jason.

Jason looked over his shoulder in each direction before returning their greeting. "Hi, how's it going? You guys working on the socials thing?"

"Yeah, we thought we should get started right away. You know, try to get it over with." Ben rationalized. "Hey, we saw George's bandage. What happened to him?"

Jason snickered softly and shook his head. "He says he got bit by a Pitt Bull." Nick and Ben tried to hide their astonishment, but couldn't resist glancing at each other. "He showed us the bite mark too. It looks really gross. It's all red and you can see where each tooth went in. He said it bled a lot."

Ben considered asking Jason if his theory about George stealing the dogs was true, but he lost his opportunity when Jason's bus pulled up at the bench. Jason said goodbye and got on the bus. The three children all began talking at once, the moment the bus pulled away. They all paused and Nick jumped in and said, "That proves it. He's the one taking the dogs. Now we just need to figure out why he's taking them and where he is keeping them."

The children huddled together on the bus stop bench talking excitedly and **speculating**.

CHAPTER SEVENTEEN

Ben and Nick headed for home when they were expected of dinner and Ricky found herself with nothing to do. She knew there was little to eat at her house and there wasn't likely to be anyone there to spend time with. The idea that had been at the back of her mind all afternoon came to the forefront. She walked the rout that she usually took to go to the Wilson's farm, but took an earlier exit from the road. She walked along a forest path and came to a clearing. She stared ahead, taking time to build courage. She had the impression that Ben and Nick went into the Mason house quite often. She had heard the stories from the kids at school about ghosts, but felt that if her new friends had come out safely, so would she. The risk would be worth the pay off for her. If she found the house to be occupy-able, she would have a dry place to hide out when her parents were fighting or when she didn't feel like going to school. She felt certain that no one would look for her at the manor house.

Ricky climbed the stairs and peeked into the front door. She whispered as she entered the foyer, "I don't mean you any harm ghosts; I'm just looking for a place to sit and read. If you don't bother me, I won't bother you."

She looked around the entry way, ready to bolt for the door the moment a ghost appeared. After a few moments she proceeded a little further into the room. She walked to a wing chair that was positioned next to the fire place and sat down. A puff of dust billowed from the cushion and the wood creaked under her weight, having sat so long in disuse. She bounced gently, testing it for comfort, shrugged slightly and dug into her backpack. She kept a flashlight with her at all times for just such occasions. When one chooses to learn away from the school setting, she found it best to do so in a very secluded place. Such places, she found, were usually a bit dark for reading.

She opened her book, drew her legs up to her chest and rested her heals on the edge of the chair. She placed her book mark on the table beside the chair and began to read. Ricky looked up from her book. Adrenaline surged through her system. She wasn't sure why, but she felt a presence in the room. She scanned the area around her and seeing nothing, looked back to the pages of her book. She read a few words then looked up again as she felt something cold brush past her arm. She moved her feet back onto the floor and slowly reached for her bag. Just as her fingers closed around the strap she heard a loud whooshing sound and light filled the room. She looked to the source of the light and discovered that a fire had sprung up in the fire place. She held her body as still as she could, watching the flames until her heart beats slowed to almost normal.

Ricky sat in the chair for almost ten minutes considering what to do. She was frightened. It was clear the house was haunted. Yet, she didn't feel threatened. The fire, it seemed to Ricky, was a sign of hospitality. "If you want me to leave, just give me a sign." she whispered. "Please don't make it a scary sign, but let me know if you don't want me here."

She waited and when it seemed that no sign was forth coming, she picked up her backpack and slung it over her shoulder. She rose from the chair and took a few tentative steps toward the stair case. "You got a nice house here. Mind if I take a look around?" she said softly. She began climbing the stairs and about half way up, she noticed a small point of light that began to glow dimly beside her. By the time she reached the top of the stair case a glowing **orb** floated by her side.

Ricky felt her heart beating harder in her chest than usual and she wondered how she had the nerve to continue walking down the dark hall. She saw a flash of movement out of the corner of her eye and she screamed as a white object streaked toward her. She ducked down to avoid being hit and crouched on the floor catching her breath. She frantically searched the room, looking for what had **accosted** her, and her eyes settled on a dim object which seemed to perch on the railing of the stairs. She squinted in the dark and leaned closer to see. She breathed an audible sigh of relief when she realized that what she was looking at was a barn owl.

The orb had disappeared during the rush of movement and Ricky looked around tentatively. She heard a sound coming from down the hall and tiptoed in the direction it seemed to come from. It grew louder as she walked closer and she soon realized that she could hear a woman humming. A chill ran down Ricky's spine as she reached a door that seemed to be the source of the eerie voice. She touched the icy door knob and found the door to be locked. The humming stopped the moment she touched the door.

She decided she had had her fill of being scared for the day and turned to leave the house. She walked back down the hall and turned down the stair case. At the bottom of the stairs she crossed the room to the front door. She turned back and looked around the room. The fire had gone out and no coals glowed in the hearth. It didn't look as if a fire had been burning there only moments ago. She turned to leave and a light suddenly appeared at the floor beside the chair she had been sitting in. She turned back and walked to the chair. She had dropped her flashlight before going upstairs. She picked it up, whispered, "Thanks, I'll come back again some time."

and walked out the door. When she saw how dark it had grown outside, she was grateful to have her flashlight for the walk home.

CHAPTER EIGHTEEN

Ricky showed up half an hour late for school Monday morning so the boys didn't get a chance to talk to her until lunchtime. The three children met at their usual spot on the playground to eat. Ben pulled a brown bag from his backpack, unfolded the top and pulled out a thick roast beef sandwich on homemade bread. Nick rummaged around in his bag until he found a bean sprout filled pita pocket. He wrinkled his nose, put the pita down and took a second look in his bag. He pulled out a twinky and smiled. Ricky pulled out a half empty bag of frosted breakfast cereal and reached in for a handful. When Nick picked up his pita and started to walk to the garbage can, Ricky stopped him and said, "If you're not going to eat that I can take care of it for you. This is good but, I had it for breakfast too." she said indicating the cereal.

"Go ahead, but you're in danger of growing long ears and whiskers from food like that." Nick passed her the sandwich.

"You know what I did after the library yesterday?" Ricky began. "I went over to that old house by your place, Ben."

Ben's eyes darted to Ricky and he **prompted** her to continue. "Did you go in?"

"I did. Those stories about it being haunted? They're definitely true. You won't believe what happened to me there."

Ricky told the boys about everything that had happened at the manor house. They were both surprised that Alexa had shown herself as much as she had. Ben still felt uncertain if he should tell Ricky about Alexa.

George and the gang showed up in the school yard after they had finished eating in the cafeteria. Ben and his friends though it would be a good idea to try to listen in on what they were saying, to get some clues as to what they were doing with the missing dogs. Ricky volunteered to try to get close enough to hear what they were saying.

She picked up Ben's paper bag and wandered off to the garbage can. After throwing it away, she began to meander around the school yard. George was talking with two of the gang boys near an opening in the fence so Ricky went across the yard on the opposite side and left the school grounds. She walked around the outside of the yard until she came to the opening where George and his friends stood. They had not noticed her, so she leaned, with her back to them, on the fence nearby.

"So you tried to get the kid's ball back, even though the dog was snarling and growling at you." Warren leaned in closer as he waited for George's reply.

"Yeah. It didn't really scare me that much. I've dealt with a lot of dogs before." He smiled smugly and continued. "It dropped the kid's ball so I grabbed it and that's when the dog got me. I gave it a good kick though and I got the kid's toy back." His friends all muttered their approval and George basked in his victory.

Just then a basket ball hit the fence near where Ricky was standing, bringing the attention of the gang boys to her presence. A couple of the boys yelled at her and kicked the fence where she stood. She backed away looking fearful, but satisfied that she had heard as much as she did.

She had a chance to tell Nick and Ben what she had heard just before the bell rang.

Nick was not satisfied with the information Ricky had gleaned because it got him no closer to recovering his missing pet. After school Ben told him that he had a plan to listen in on the gang, but that they would have to give Ricky the slip in order for it to work. When she came walking in their direction Ben whispered, "Meet me near

Miss Crumbey's house." before she could hear.

"What are you two up to?" Ricky inquired.

"I have a lot of homework." Ben lied. "I need to get home and get started. How about you Nick?"

"My mom told me to come straight home and clean my room after school. So I better get going. See you guys tomorrow." Nick felt guilty when he noticed Ricky's disappointment, but walked away quickly.

Nick met Ben in front of Miss Crumbey's house and Ben indicated that they should walk up the forest path. As the boys neared the gang's gathering place, Ben pulled the cord that held the key from around his neck. Ben told Nick to wait and watch for the gang boys while he ran into the clearing and hung the key on a branch in an **inconspicuous** place. He rubbed the key and whispered a few words then turned and walked away. Just as Ben stepped out of view, three of the gang boys walked into the clearing holding a large cardboard box. Ben and Nick watched as more of the boys gathered and began to remove things from the box. The boys saw Colin pick up a bottle of baby powder and strained to see what the other boys pulled from the box.

As Nick stretched his neck to try to get a better look he felt a hand grip the back of his shirt. "What are you two doing here again!" Tommy yelled.

Nick squirmed out of Tommy's grasp and he and

Ben ran from the forest with Tommy in pursuit. Soon Tommy gave up the chase and headed back to the forest while Ben and Nick stopped to catch their breath.

"I'll have to go back for the key." Ben panted. "I'm going to hide at Miss Crumbey's house until I see them leave and then I'll go back and get it."

They walked back to Miss Crumbey's house and quickly ducked behind the shrubs beside the front porch. The boys saw the old woman lean out her front door. She struggled down the stairs and began poking around in the shrubs. "Who's out here? I saw you kids sneaking around my house again. You better not be trying to scare my cats."

Nick grabbed Ben's arm and tugged him down to the ground. Ben watched as Nick shuffled along the dirt ground and disappeared into the darkness. He followed behind Nick and found himself hidden in the darkness beneath Miss Crumbey;s front porch. The boys waited silently in Ricky's hiding place until they heard Miss Crumbey's cane thumping back up the stairs and into the house. They waited a few minutes more until they were sure the coast was clear and began to crawl out of their hiding place.

"What's this?" Ben muttered as his hand **encountered** an object in the dark. He picked it up and shuffled out into the light. He held up the object to show Nick and was surprised to see the colour drain from

Nick's face.

"That's Rufus's collar!" Nick grabbed it from Ben's hand and examined it more closely. He held the dog tag between his fingers and peered at the words engraved on it. "It really is Rufus's." Nick seemed to be near tears and struggled to contain himself. He stuffed the collar in his backpack and the boys settled in to wait silently.

Half an hour later they watched some of the gang boys emerge from the forest. They waited a while longer to be certain they were all gone, and then Ben and Nick ran to the path. They crept quietly to the clearing and found the area to be abandoned. Ben walked to the tree he had hung the key from and reached to the spot he expected to find it. He turned to Nick wearing a startled expression, then dropped to his hands and knees and began to frantically feel around in the twigs and leaves on the ground.

"It's not there?" Nick's voice was strained. He joined Ben in his search of the ground.

After picking through every twig and leaf the boys finally had to admit to themselves that the key was gone. They walked from the forest, both wearing a bleak expression and walked separately to their homes.

CHAPTER NINETEEN

Ricky didn't show up at school the following day and both Ben and Nick were quiet and disheartened about the loss of the key. They kept a close watch on the gang boys who had been present in the clearing the day before to see if any of them was in possession of the key. They planned to go to Mason Manor after school. Ben wondered if Alexa would still appear to him without the key and he wondered how angry she would be that he had lost it.

Ricky had felt rejected when her new friends had brushed her off the day before. When she woke up she found that her dad was already gone and her mother was still sleeping. She couldn't bear the thought of spending the day at school so she packed her book, flashlight and what food she could scrape together into her backpack and left the house. She was a little nervous about it, but she knew where she was going to spend the day. She headed straight for Mason Manor.

Ricky walked onto the porch of the house and peeked tentatively into the front door. There appeared to be nothing to be frightened of so she walked in. The novel Ricky was reading was at a very exciting point so, though she was tempted to explore the house a bit, she decided to sit in the same chair she had used before and read a chapter or two. This would also be wise, she thought, because it would allow for a quick exit, should anything scary happen. She placed her bag on the floor beside the chair and rummaged through it in search of her book and her flashlight. When she found what she was looking for she turned to sit in the chair. She jumped and turned back in the direction she had been facing before. She thought she had seen a movement out of the corner of her eye. Seeing nothing obvious, she assumed that her imagination was playing tricks on her. She settled onto the chair and opened her book. Again she caught a movement to her left and she turned to see only empty space.

When her reading was distracted a third time, she decided to put her book away and explore the house a little. She tucked the book back into her bag, but kept the flashlight out. She slung the backpack over her shoulder and took a step toward the stairs when she stopped suddenly. There was someone standing on the stairs. She fumbled with the flashlight and, in her rush, dropped it. By the time she picked it up, turned it on and shone it on the stairs, there was no one there. Ricky contemplated leaving the house, but she knew that by this point, attendance had been taken at school and the **truancy** officer would have her name on a list. She couldn't risk finding a new place to hide out for the day.

Ricky walked up the stairs aware of a feeling of being watched. She resisted the urge to turn around and look behind her. "You're not as friendly today are you?" she whispered. "I mean you no harm. I just need a place to hide for the day. Please don't scare me."

She reached the top of the stairs and began walking down the hall. She walked past the door where she had heard the singing the last time. She felt compelled to go to the room at the end of the hall. When she reached the door and looked inside she realized why. It was a library. The room was somewhat brighter than the other rooms and she could see dust particles floating in the air. A beam of light shone into the room from a small dirty window and **illuminated** what Ricky considered to be a priceless treasure. There were stacks and stacks of books. The young girl stood with mouth agape and eyes wide, turning to take in the room. She took a few steps and picked up a book from the top of a pile that had fallen from a shelf. She held it a moment then gingerly wiped the dust from the title. She opened the book and was relieved to see that the pages were still intact. She placed the book on an empty shelf and continued to walk around the room, picking up books, studying them a moment then putting down again. She found a large hard cover book lying open on a desk at the back of the room. The page it was open to was so faded that Ricky couldn't make out the words. She gently turned one of the brittle pages and read a few lines. *"By the pricking of my thumbs, Something wicked this way comes: Open, locks, Whoever knocks!"* Shakespeare; she recognized. She picked up the book and walked back to the leather couch that was in front of the library door. She sat down and began to read.

She lost track of how long she had been reading until she felt the first pangs of hunger. She reached into her bag and pulled out a plastic wrapped stack of crackers. She ate as she continued to read. When she had had her fill of crackers, she pulled her legs up onto the couch, rested her head on the arm support and closed her eyes.

As she slept she heard a voice whisper in her head, "You like books. I like to read too. You are reading the book that I was reading. You have something that doesn't belong to you. Where did you get it? You must give it back."

She heard these words over and over in her sleep. "Where did you get it? You must give it back. You have something..."

Ricky awoke with a start. She had heard a noise. She felt dazed from her sleep and confused about where she was. She could still hear the hollow voice echoing in her head. "You have something... You must give it back."

She jumped up and ran from the room. Moving from the dim light of the library into the darkness of the hall, her eyes felt blind. She walked into a wall, banging her head, confusing her even more. She panicked when she realized that she had left her backpack and her flashlight back in the library. She ran down the hall, not sure which direction she was going and not sure what she was running from. She felt the banister of the grand stair case and followed it until her foot stumbled down a few stairs. She scrambled to gain her footing and began to run down the stairs. At the bottom of the stair case she could see the dim light from the crack of the front door and she ran for it. Before she got there she ran into something which stopped her in her tracks. She screamed as arms closed around her shoulders.

"Ricky! Is that you?" She heard Ben's familiar voice. "What are you doing here? What are you scared of?"

Ricky collapsed against Ben chest; panting, sobbing and wiping her tears. He hugged her and spoke to her in a soothing voice. Nick placed his hand on her back and said, "Are you okay Ricky? We are with you now. You're alright."

She stepped back from Ben, took a deep breath and spoke. "I'm okay now. I don't know why I was so frightened. I fell asleep and someone was talking to me.

She scared me I guess. It was just a dream, but it was kind of scary. What time is it? Is school out already?"

"Yeah, where were you?" Nick asked.

"I didn't feel like going today. I came here. I've been in the library reading all day. I just had a bad dream." She rubbed her eyes then suddenly stiffened her back and stared at Ben. "Hey, what did you two do after school yesterday? Did you go to the woods near Miss Crumbey's house after you both told me you were going home?"

"We did." Ben looked to the ground and kicked a stone at his feet. "How did you know?"

"I found something. I forgot I even had it. I think it's in my backpack, upstairs in the library. Come with me." Ricky turned toward the stairs, but glanced over her shoulder to double check that the boys were following.

When they reached the library, Ricky found her bag lying on the floor beside the couch as she had left it. She reached in and rummaged around at the bottom. She extracted her hand and held the object out to Ben. It was the key!

Ben reached for it. "The key! Why do you have it?" he asked.

"I went up to the clearing to spy on those guys to see if I could find out anything about Nick's dog. They were just leaving when I got there, but I saw your key hanging in the tree and I wondered if they had stolen it from you." she explained. "I forgot that I even had it or I guess I would have gone to school today to bring it to you."

Ben lifted the cord over his head, strung it around his neck and tucked the key back into his shirt. He mumbled, "I'm sorry I lost it Alexa. That must be why she was scaring you." Ben explained to Ricky, forgetting that they hadn't told her about the ghost yet.

"You've got it back now, so it's alright." Alexa's voice sounded hollow and distant. "I'm sorry for scaring your friend. I didn't know why she had my key."

The voice seemed, to Ricky, to come from everywhere in the room. She felt the same chill and feeling of dread come over her that had caused her to run last time.

"I think you're scaring her again, Alexa." Ben scolded. "You wouldn't be so scary if you were visible. Why don't you appear?"

Ricky was stunned as she watched a young girl materialize in front of her. She looked like an ordinary girl, although she was dressed in old fashion clothes and wore her long dark hair in a thick braid. She didn't look like a ghost. She looked as solid as Ben or Nick, but the way she had appeared out of nowhere convinced Ricky that she was not a real person. Ricky looked wary.

"This is Alexa, Ricky. This is her house. We're trying to help her figure out why she hasn't moved on to the afterlife." Ben told her.

Ricky smiled weakly, but still looked frightened.

"You don't need to be afraid of me." Alexa said. "I won't hurt you. I don't think I could hurt anything if I wanted to. I've been practicing trying to move things," she looked at Ben dismayed, "but I haven't had any success."

"You did move something just the other day though!" Ben retorted. "Remember when that bag of vegetables fell off the stairs, Ricky? That was you Alexa; I'm sure of it. What were you thinking at the time?"

"I was thinking about how I had put you in an awkward position. I thought that if I could just kick that bag off the stairs, it would be a good distraction. I didn't think it was me who had moved it. Do you really think I did that?"

"I know you did. Now, I have to ask you something." Ben changed the subject. He was excited to find out if their plan had worked the previous day. "Did you realize that I had put the key in the woods yesterday, so you could try to listen in on the gang boys?"

"Yes," Alexa answered, "I felt you take it off. I

felt sad and lonely when you didn't have it. Like I felt before you picked it up." Alexa's shoulders slumped and she looked as if she might start to cry.

"I'm sorry you felt bad." Ben patted the key on his chest. "We did agree to try doing that though, Right?"

Alexa nodded and Ben continued. "Were you able to hear them? Did they say anything useful?"

"I could hear them just as well as I can hear you right now!" Alexa perked up and began to look excited. "That boy Tommy, he wanted to see George's wound." Alexa wrinkled her nose. "George was quite proud to show it off. I didn't want to look, but I'm glad I did. I've seen a dog bite before and that wasn't a dog bite." Alexa's tone was very matter of fact. "I whispered to Tommy that it wasn't a dog bite. I knew I was taking a bit of a risk doing that, but I didn't like George pulling the wool over his eyes. George is not a very nice person. It worked too. I don't think Tommy even knew it wasn't his own thought." Alexa smiled mischievously. "He told George that he didn't believe it was a dog bite. George admitted that it wasn't. He confessed to Tommy that it was his baby brother that bit him. He made Tommy promise not to tell anyone that he had lied."

"It's not a dog bite?" Nick deflated with a sigh. "Now we're no further ahead than we were before"

"Either way," Ben said, "it's better to know the

truth. If it turns out they're not the ones taking the dogs, we wouldn't want to accuse them. Besides, maybe we should be focusing on Miss. Crumbey. We did find Rufus's collar under her porch."

"That was your dog's collar?" Ricky interjected.

"Yes. What do you know about it?" Nick said.

"I found it on the sidewalk in front of her house. I picked it up and bought it under the porch. I meant to show it to you guys, but I forgot all about it."

"So it wasn't Miss Crumbey who put it under the porch." Ben said. "That makes it less suspicious, but it doesn't mean she's off the hook. Same goes for George. Either one of them still could be the thief. We just have to keep watching them."

The three children and their ghostly friend settled in to make some plans to get to the bottom of the dogs' disappearances.

CHAPTER TWENTY

After a planning session to solve the dog mystery, Nick reminded Ben about their original reason for coming to the house. They had intended to spend some time searching the rooms of the house for clues to Alexa's past. Ricky eagerly offered to help and the children moved from the library to the hall. They stood outside of the room they had searched last and asked Alexa which room they should move on to.

"The next room is mine. It's locked. I can go in, but you three can't and I can't move anything around. I think our best hope of finding answers is in there, but it will have to wait. Maybe we will find the key in another room." She took a few steps further down the hall and stopped. "This is my mother's room. I was forbidden to go in here unless my mother asked me in. I don't feel right about searching in here." She moved to continue down the hall, but Ben's voice stopped her.

"If you really want to find some answers we're going to have to search the whole house. The answers you're looking for could be just behind this door. When is the last time you went in this room?"

"I haven't gone in there. Not since my mother was here to invite me in." She looked puzzled. "Now that I think about it, it's probably silly that I've continued to abide by rules that were set by someone who has been gone for so long. I've spent decades doing nothing but follow old routines that I had in my lifetime. It was never my habit to go into that room, so I've never gone in."

"So the answer to your mystery could just be sitting there in that room." Nick marvelled. "It could be just laying there on a table waiting to be discovered."

"Are you ready to do this?" Ben asked Alexa. He was excited, but he wanted to be sensitive to Alexa's feelings. She hadn't changed her ways in over a hundred years and he didn't want to rush her into doing something that would make her uncomfortable.

"Let's go." She said firmly and led the way into the room. The room was filled with frilly and lacy things. It was obviously a lady's room.

Nick bustled into the room and began to open and close drawers on a vanity table, quickly glancing at the contents and dismissing them as **irrelevant**. Ben laid a **restraining** hand on Nick's shoulder and nodded toward

Alexa. Alexa walked slowly around the room looking at objects, reaching out to touch them, then pulling her hand back when she realized that touching was something she was **incapable** of. Her face wore a dreamy, sad expression. She looked as though she might cry. The three children stood silently waiting for a sign that Alexa was ready to begin the search. "I'm sorry." she said as she came to the realization that everyone was waiting for her."I guess I miss my mother more than I realized. We had some special times together in this room. She would fix my hair for parties while I sat at that vanity. Sometimes we would both snuggle into her bed on cold nights and read books to each other. I used to love to come in this room." She sighed deeply and continued, "Let's get started."

Nick continued searching the vanity while Ben looked in a tall chest of drawers and Ricky looked through the night stand. Alexa stood by watching wistfully as her friends searched her mother's room.

Ricky finished searching the night stand and moved to look under the bed. She pulled out a large wooden box with a hinged lid and blew a thick layer of dust from the lid. The hinges creaked as she lifted the top and all of the children turned to see what had made the sound. The box was filled to the top with yellowed crumbling papers and envelopes. "Letters!" Ricky said "This could be useful. We should read through all of these. You never know what we'll find."

"Let's each take a bunch to read and share anything that seems useful. Here," Ben said taking the top letter from the box. "I'll lay this one out on the bed for you, Alexa, so you can help too." He gently pulled the fragile letter from its envelope and unfolded the papers. He laid each page side by side across the bed for Alexa to read then took a few letters from the box to read himself.

"This letter is from Isabell Brachan. Who is that Alexa?" Nick questioned.

"That's my aunt; my mother's sister. Is there something useful in the letter?"

"She suggests that you might have run away and asks if you and your mother had argued. I wish we had the letters your mother wrote too. It's a bit hard to understand a one sided conversation. She seems to be comforting your mother and says you'll probably come back soon." Nick turned to face Alexa. "Did you run away from home?"

"Not that I can remember. Certainly I would remember something like that. I would have been missing for weeks if my mother wrote to her sister in Montreal and received a reply letter about it."

"Oh!" Ricky interjected. "This letter says that you had been missing for over a month. It's dated September nineteenth, eighteen ten. What is the date on that letter, Nick?"

"September fifth." he responded. "You did go missing then. For at least a month. You don't remember anything about that?"

"No!" Alexa sat on the bed looking as though she had received shocking news. "If I went missing, my mother would have been **devastated**. It is no wonder I hear her crying all the time. I wonder if I ever came back." She looked at Ben as though she had been startled. "Do you think that I never came back? Is that why I don't remember?" She paused, looking more and more shocked as reality dawned on her. "Do you think I died?"

"Let's not jump to conclusions." Ben refolded the letter he had been reading and tucked it back into its envelope. "We do have to be realistic though. You are a spirit, not a flesh and blood person. You are a ghost," he restated it in case it wasn't perfectly clear, "and you are a ghost for a reason. You must have died **traumatically**. That's what I've been reading; that ghosts were people who died traumatically and that's why their spirit isn't at peace."

"It's starting to make sense." Nick nodded slowly. "You went missing. Maybe you had an accident, maybe you were murdered; but your mom didn't know. If she had no closure, maybe you couldn't move on because she was so upset. Does that make sense?"

"It does, but we don't have the facts yet." Ricky tried to be rational. "We should read through the rest of these letters and gather all the information we can from them. Then we should keep searching the house. If we found this information here, who knows what else we might find. I think Alexa is right, that her room could hold the answers. We need to get in there." An idea dawned on Ricky. "Ben did you try your key on Alexa's door?"

"I already tried it. It fits in the lock, but it doesn't open the door. I just realized though, the key must be a big piece of the puzzle. Why else would Alexa be so connected to it?"

All of them nodded their agreement. "We should keep reading and keep searching the house." Ricky said. "Maybe the lock for the key is in the house and that will give us the answer."

Ben turned to Alexa. "Have you thought about what finding the answer means? I'm guessing that when we figure out what happened to you, you will be able to move on. You would be gone. How do you feel about that?"

"Before I met you three, I would have said I had nothing else keeping me here. It is nice to have friends and to break the cycle of going through the motions that I was in. Really though, I am tired of this existence. If I can't be a real person with a real life, I should move on. It is the natural order of things. I always have this feeling of anguish too. I would like to have some peace."

"Alright, it's settled then. We'll do whatever it takes to find out what happened to you, Alexa. Let's make a pact; the four of us, to get to the bottom of this." Ben stated rather **ceremoniously**.

"To find out what happened to Alexa," Nick reiterated, "and to find out what's happening to the dogs. I know the dogs aren't as important as Alexa, but can we still work on that too?"

"Of course, Nick," Alexa said "and I'll help in any way that I can to figure out what happened to your dog."

"A pact then." Ben held his right hand out in front of him, open with his palm facing down. Ricky stepped forward and placed her open hand on top of Ben's. Nick followed suit and Alexa stepped into the circle they had formed. She held her hand in a similar fashion, but hesitated to place it on the hands of the others. Ben nodded his head to encourage Alexa and nodded toward their stacked hands. Alexa took a step forward and placed her hand on top of the pile. "We swear to find the answers to these mysteries together." Ben said solemnly. "We will be loyal to this group and we will work tirelessly until we have all the answers." He paused, then said simply, "I swear."

"I swear." Ricky vowed.

"I swear." Nick repeated.

"I swear." Alexa whispered softly, overcome by

emotion.

CHAPTER TWENTY-ONE

Early Saturday afternoon, Ben closed his binder, tucked it into his backpack and headed downstairs for lunch. It was a rainy October day and the smell of homemade soup and fresh baked bread welcomed him when he entered the kitchen. Gran smiled and asked about his homework as she cut a thick slice of brown bread and ladled a bowl of steaming hot soup for him.

"I've just about finished my research project on ghosts. I just need to print it out and glue the illustrations in. I think I'll get a really good mark."

"You should have asked all your ghost friends over at the house to help you on that project. You could have had some firsthand information for Mr. Weir." Gran said.

Ben's eyes were wide with shock. "My friends, Gran?" he asked. How could she know, he wondered?

"Well, you spend so much time there; I thought you must have made friends with the ghosts that haunt that house by now. That place is becoming a regular clubhouse for you and your flesh and blood friends." Gran smiled and nudged Ben in the arm with her elbow.

"Oh Gran, you're pulling my leg." Ben laughed with relief. "It's a pretty cool place to hang out. There is a lot of stuff still in there. Why didn't anyone ever clear out all the stuff and how come no one ever moved in there after the Mason's left?"

"No one has lived in that house for over a hundred years." Gran began. "I think it was just forgotten about for a long time. When we bought the property, it had **reverted** to government ownership because there were no heirs claiming it for so long. I don't think anyone made note of the fact that that old house was even there. The locals knew about it, but there was so much folk lore about its being haunted that everyone just stayed away from it.

"I made some inquiries before we bought it, though. That was almost fifty years ago. I didn't want anyone coming along claiming it was theirs after your grandfather and I had settled in. I found an old woman in town, Mrs. Markham; she was well into her nineties when I spoke to her. She remembered hearing a bit about the Mason family from her grandmother when she was a child.

"It seems that the Masons were a very well to do

family at one time. They had servants and relatives living in the house with them, but they only ever had one child, as far as far as old Mrs. Markham's grandmother could remember. They were famous for hosting grand parties and inviting everyone in town. Mrs. Markham said her grandmother remembered going there a couple of times as a very young child. She said that it was magical. They would decorate the house **elaborately** according to whatever the season was. She said there was so much food that she left with a stomach ache. The servants would walk around with trays of food and drinks. They had a little orchestra playing music. Those parties were the highlight of her childhood.

"Something changed suddenly though. Apparently Mrs. Mason went a little funny when she was still relatively young. She never went out and they stopped having guests. It seems that after Mr. Mason died, the place went into ruin and Mrs. Mason lived there alone for a long time. Mrs. Markham didn't know what had happened to the daughter either. She didn't come to take care of her mother in the end. Mrs. Mason stayed in the house until she died. The will left everything to the daughter, but she never claimed it.

"I suppose having a crazy old hermit woman living alone in such a big house till she died, lends itself to ghost stories. I was surprised at everything that was left in the house too. I would have thought that thieves would have cleaned it out long ago. I guess it's just so far removed from town that no one ever got out to the house."

"Wow! It's a good thing you found out about those things before Mrs. Markham died." Ben was excited to hear even some small details about the history of the house. "If she hadn't told you, all that history would be lost. You should write down everything she told you. Maybe Nick and Ricky and I can find out more about what happened by looking through all the stuff in the house."

"That sound like a worthwhile project." Gran said. She was impressed that Ben was taking such an interest in history. Ben was happy to have an excuse for why he and his friends were spending so much time going through the contents of the house.

Ben was suddenly startled by frantic knocking at the door. Gran went out into the back porch to answer the door and Ricky came flying into the kitchen ahead of Gran looking like she was ready to burst. She almost began talking, but when Gran walked in the room she pursed her lips tightly and sat stiffly on the stool beside Ben.

"I'll get you some soup, Ricky, but then I've got some things to attend to. I'll have to leave the two of you alone and get on with my chores." Grandmother excused herself sensing that Ricky wanted urgently to speak to Ben alone.

As soon as Gran was out of earshot, Ricky began to whisper to Ben. "The Wilson's have a book about breeding dogs! " She stared at Ben expectantly.

"So..." Ben prompted her.

"So!?" she implored dramatically. "Don't you see? They could be the ones stealing the dogs! I saw the book on Mr. Wilson's desk when Mrs. Wilson asked me to bring a file of receipts into the house and put it in the office."

"Why does their having a book about breeding dogs make you think they are the ones stealing all the dogs?"

"Oh Ben, think about it." Ricky held up her hands with her palms to the ceiling. "They don't even own a dog. What would they want a book about breeding dogs for? I bet they're stealing dogs to breed them!" She smiled eagerly as if it should all make sense to him now.

"I think you're jumping to conclusions. You're the one that's all rational about the Alexa thing and now you're flying off the handle because the Wilsons have a book. It doesn't make sense. What would they want so many dogs for? I thought you liked the Wilson's so much?"

"I do! I wish Mrs. Wilson was my mom, but if they're doing something wrong; something that's hurting people like Nick, I don't want them to get away with it.

Why are you so against believing that it could be them?"

"I guess that I've been thinking that it was George's gang for so long now that it's hard for me to consider other possibilities. I've never really believed that Miss Crumbey was a suspect either. I will try to keep an open mind, but don't jump to conclusions either." Ben said.

"Let's talk to Alexa and Nick about it and see what they think." Ricky persisted.

Ben phoned Nick and made arrangements to meet him at the manor house later. Ricky and Ben finished their lunch and walked over to the house. Alexa had just appeared when Nick walked in the door. Ricky told them about the dog breeding book. Nick seemed almost as **sceptical** as Ben, but Alexa had a suggestion.

"Why don't we listen in on both them and the gang and see if there is more we can find out. Hide the key somewhere that they will think they are alone and I will listen for clues."

"Are you willing to take that risk again, even after I almost lost the key that way last time?" Ben said.

"You didn't actually almost lose the key. You just felt like you did because you didn't know it was Ricky who had it. We have to do something. Do you have any other suggestions?" Alexa asked.

When Ben could come up with no alternative, they began making plans.

Ben arrived early at school the next day. He removed a roll of masking tape from his backpack and headed straight to the cafeteria. The gang had a regular table that they sat at for lunch and there was not a single student at the school who would consider beating them to the spot. Ben scanned the room to make sure there was no one there watching, then crouched down beside the table. He removed the leather cord from his neck and untied the knot. He put the empty cord in his pocket and taped the key to the underside of the table.

The day dragged by for Ben, who was nervous about the key. At lunchtime he insisted on eating in the cafeteria so that he could watch the table and keep an eye on the key. Nick purposely left his backpack in the cafeteria when they went back to class for the afternoon. At the end of the day the three children loitered around the school until most of the students and staff had left. Nick called his dad's cell phone, told him that he had forgotten his bag in the cafeteria and asked if he would let him in to go get it.

Mr. Follows met Nick at the side entrance to the

school and let him in. Nick ran down the hall to the cafeteria and went straight to the gang table. He got down on his knees and peered under the table. He removed the wad of masking tape and was relieved to find the key was still there. As soon as he touched the key he heard Alexa's voice echo inside of his head.

"I learned something useful, but I don't think it has anything to do with the dogs. Go to the house so I can tell you all."

Back at the manor house Nick handed Ben the key. After Ben had strung the key around his neck Alexa appeared to them looking quite excited. "The gang boys are planning a prank." she said. "That's what they have been working on up in the forest by Miss Crumbey's. They're planning to play a trick on your teacher. They have something... I think a balloon. It's filled with powder and they are going to put it in his desk drawer. When he opens his drawer, it is supposed to burst and puff the white powder all over his face."

"That's why we saw them with the baby powder in the clearing. It sounds like a pretty harmless prank, but it would be embarrassing for Mr. Weir." Ben said. "It might be kind of fun to figure out a way to make it backfire on them. When are they planning to pull this off?"

"They're setting it up today. It will happen

tomorrow as soon as your teacher opens his drawer."

"Let's go over to the school. I bet my dad will help us re-rig their booby trap."

CHAPTER TWENTY-TWO

The next morning Ben didn't see Nick on the school grounds. He worried that their plan to inform Mr. Weir about the prank would be too late. The bell rang and Ben took a last look around for Nick before walking into the school. Ben walked by just in time to see Nick leaving the school office. He gave a slight nod to Ben and they proceeded to class. Both boys were surprised to see Ricky arrive at school on time for a change.

All three children waited eagerly to see how the **double-cross** would play out. When they had completed their morning assignments and nothing had happened they began to wonder if Mr. Weir was simply going to let George get away with his disrespectful plan. The day wore on and the friends grew impatient with the wait.

Just before lunch, Mr. Weir was writing on the chalk board when his chalk broke, most **spectacularly**, and fell to the floor shattering into many little pieces. He made a bit of a production of cleaning it up and walking to his desk to get a new piece. Ben knew from the work they had done with Mr. Follows the night before, that the desk drawer that was supposed to have been booby-trapped was the one where Mr. Weir kept his chalk. Mr. Weir paused dramatically, then opened his drawer and uneventfully pulled out a new piece of chalk. Ben heard a couple of George's friends make small gasps and sounds of disappointment.

Mr. Weir resumed writing on his board and, with his back still toward the class, commented that he needed a chalk **compass**. "George, there's one in the drawer right beside you. Will you be kind enough to grab it for me?"

George shrugged, stood and walked to the drawer. "This drawer?" he asked. Mr. Weir nodded and George grasped the drawer pull. The drawer seemed to stick a little the first time he tried to open it, so he pulled again with more force. The drawer resisted a moment then suddenly **yielded** and sprang open. There was popping sound and a **plume** of white dust burst into the air and covered George's face. He paused, and then began to sneeze. The class erupted with laughter and Mr. Weir, uncharacteristically, joined in. When George finally stopped sneezing he wiped his sleeve across his nose, leaving a white streak on his black shirt. He looked up at the class who was staring at him and everyone burst into laughter anew. The place George had wiped clean of white powder under his nose looked just like a pig's snout. It stood out very clearly because, other than two circles around his eyes, the pig snout was the only part of George's face that was pink, rather than glaringly white. Ben noticed that as the class continued to laugh, the snout changed from pink to red.

At lunch time the three friends gathered at their usual eating place. Ricky held three small, wrinkled apples. She sighed deeply and bit into one. Ben guessed that there had been no food in her house again and she had made a detour on the way to school to pick apples off the tree beside the river. He reached into his bag with the intention of making an excuse that he did not like the kind of sandwich that his grandmother had made, and giving it to her. To his satisfaction he found that Gran had packed two sandwiches. "Gran sent two sandwiches, Ricky. Do you want one?"

"Oh, sure." She tried to sound casual, but looked hungrily at the food. Ben handed it to her and she tore into it with great **relish**. "This is so good, Ben." She sputtered. "I had apples for breakfast too, so I really appreciate this."

"I wish she had packed three." Nick said and took a small bite of a lumpy looking greenish loaf of **undistinguishable** origin. He rewrapped the item and tossed it into the trash can. "Trust me, Ricky. Even you wouldn't have wanted to eat that. Let's see if there is anything in here from Max." Nick felt around in his bag, smiled and pulled out a three pack of butter tarts. He ate two and gave one to Ricky. The children reviewed the plan they had made with Alexa the previous evening. They were so happy with how their spy tactic had worked out with George's gang that they felt confident that it would work well with the Wilson's too.

After school the three friends walked to the Mason house together. They spoke briefly with Alexa then put their plan into action. Nick handed Ricky a roll of masking tape and a small **skein** of string while Ben removed the key cord from his neck. He removed the leather cord and held the key a moment. "It feels weird to have this off. Come back to me soon." He spoke to the key like it was a friend and handed it to Ricky.

As Ricky walked away from her friends, Ben called out to her. "Come to my house when you're done there. You can let me know how it went and Gran will get you some dinner."

The next day the children followed the same routine after school, only Alexa didn't appear to them at the Mason house. Ricky headed off to the Wilson's farm with the plan to return to Ben's house with the key later.

Ben expected Ricky around dinner time, so while he cleared the dinner plates from the table he noticed an uncomfortable feeling growing in his stomach. He knew that something had to have gone wrong for it to take Ricky so long to return with the key. He went upstairs to begin his homework with a sense of foreboding building inside of him.

He was just finishing his math assignment and putting the text book back into his school bag when he heard tapping on his window. His heart was pounding, both from being startled by the window knock and from the dread he felt over what Ricky was about to say. Ben walked to the glass and knelt on the window seat as he unlatched the lock. He slid the window open and searched Ricky's face for a clue as to what she had found out. Though he was half expecting it, he was disappointed by the look of dread on her face.

"It wasn't there." she whispered. "I put it up on a high shelf in the office and when I went back to get it today, it wasn't there! I hung around for a long time to see if it turned up anywhere, but it didn't! I didn't know what to do." She was so upset that she looked near tears.

Although Ben felt nearly as frantic as Ricky appeared, he tried to stay calm. He knew it would only make things worse if one of them wasn't level headed. "Could it have fallen off the shelf? Did you check the floor under the shelf?"

"I did check. It wasn't there. What are we going to do Ben?"

"We are going to stay calm and think about this. Did you tape the key to the shelf?" He asked.

"No; I thought that would look too suspicious if they found it."

"That was good thinking. So someone has the key, but they obviously don't know what it's for. You need to hang around there as much as you can tomorrow because somebody is eventually going to ask someone what the key is for. Depending on who has the key, you could tell them it was yours and that you lost it."

"Yeah if Mrs. Wilson has it I could try that, but if it's Mr. Wilson I don't think he'll believe that. Do you think Alexa will be able to help us get the key back?" Ricky said.

"I hope she will, but I don't really know. I'm starting to wonder if she can appear to us at the house if we don't have the key. Nick and I should go there tomorrow and see if we can bring her out, while you go to the farm and try to find out what you can about the key. Just let me go down stairs and grab you something to eat before you get going."

Ben was putting together a sandwich for Ricky when his grandmother came into the kitchen holding a paper bag. "Put some fruit and a few of those muffins in for her too, Ben. Might as well make sure she has something to eat at breakfast time tomorrow."

Ben added the food to the bag his grandmother had supplied and brought it up to Ricky. After she left he phoned Nick to inform him of the situation, then he called his dad.

For the first few weeks Ben had lived at his grandparents' house, he had talked with his father almost daily. The phone calls had dropped off to every other day for a while and now he was finding it difficult to call at a time his father would answer the phone. Ben calculated that it had been nearly a week since he had spoken to his dad. Ben let the phone ring until the voice mail picked up and he left a brief message.

The next day the children met after school and walked to Mason Manor. Nick suggested that Ricky should come in at least for a few minutes while they tried to bring forth Alexa. If they were able to speak to Alexa she might be able to tell them where Ricky should look for the key.

Ben knocked on the door and the three children walked into the house. Ben called out to Alexa a few times and then Ricky suggested that they should look for her in the library at this time of day. They all took turns calling Alexa's name on the way upstairs and continued to call out to her in the library. After a few minutes they agreed that the effort was wasted and that Ricky should move her efforts to the Wilson farm.

Ricky walked to the farm feeling **apprehensive** in spite of the beautiful fall weather. She felt somewhat torn in her loyalty between her two sets of friends. Mrs. Wilson had been giving her food and checking on her well being for a couple of years now. In fact she had become more of a mother to her than her own mother had been recently. On the other hand, she had always had difficulty making friends at school and Ben and Nick were turning out to be two of the best friends she had ever had. She hated to be disloyal to Mrs. Wilson, but she wanted to help solve the dog problem. She walked up to the barn praying that the Wilsons were not the ones stealing the dogs.

Ricky heard the jingle of metal that could only be a set of keys, as she walked into the barn. Mr. Wilson was just unlocking a cabinet that Ricky had never seen inside of before. She stepped silently into the shadows and waited in hopes of learning something useful.

"Come on, Jane. Just get the medicine into the cabinet before that kid shows up. If you're going to keep trying to mother her, you're going to have to figure out a way to keep her from figuring out what we are doing here."

"She won't figure anything out." Mrs. Wilson replied. "We are covering our tracks very well. Help me get this case of **syringes** onto the top shelf and then you can lock up."

As they locked the cupboard, Ricky stepped out of the shadows and walked into the room. "Hi." She tried to hide the nervousness in her voice. "What do you need help with today, Mrs. Wilson?"

"Oh, hi Ricky!" Mrs. Wilson was startled to see Ricky walk in. "You can refill the produce baskets. Grab yourself a snack out of there too, hun. You'll have to get the keys from Mr. Wilson though. We've just come back from the city and everything is locked up still."

Ricky stepped up to Mr. Wilson with her hand extended and he dropped his keys into her palm. She let out a little yelp and dropped the keys onto the dirt floor. Something had stung her palm. She bent down to pick up the keys and gasped as she recognized Alexa's silver skeleton key gleaming amongst the modern keys that filled Mr. Wilson's key chain. She snatched up the keys and ran to the building where the produce was kept, trying to buy herself time to think before she acted.

She was tempted to just remove the key from the ring and run back to the manor house, but she knew that that behaviour would draw too much suspicion. If she took the key and gave the key chain back to Mr. Wilson, he would surely notice within moments that the fancy key was missing.

As she stood in the shed worrying over what to do, a familiar voice whispered inside of her ears. *"I have an idea. I will need your help."*

"Alexa!" Ricky whispered. "We've been so worried! How will we get the key back?"

"I don't want to take the time to explain it all now; it will be too suspicious if you take too long. I'm going to try something I've never done before. Go back out, prepared to do the work you're expected to do. Make sure Mrs. Wilson is there when you give the keys back to Mr.Wilson. Ask him about the silver key. Go now." Alexa prompted Ricky.

Ricky picked up a basket of carrots, took a bite from one, as she normally would and walked out of the shed. Mr. Wilson was still talking to his wife so she set down the basket and walked over to return the keys. Ricky held the heavy set of keys up in front of Mr. Wilson and he took them from her hand. Ricky noticed Mrs. Wilson jump slightly as though someone had startled her and then go slack as though she was asleep standing up. Her facial expression was completely blank. Ricky tore her eyes from the woman and said to Mr. Wilson. "What's that big silver key on your key chain?"

"I don't honestly know, Ricky. I was actually

meaning to ask Mrs. Wilson if she knew what it was for. I just found it in my office the other day." Mr. Wilson answered. "Do you know what it is Jane?"

Mrs. Wilson turned stiffly to her husband and said in a very flat voice, "It's nothing really. Just something I was planning to give to Ricky."

Ricky was feeling a little confused, but followed her **instinct** and replied, "That would be lovely, Mrs. Wilson!" She feared she sounded like a bad actress. "All the kids are starting to wear keys as jewellery. I was just wishing I had something like that."

Mr. Wilson shrugged, removed the key from his key chain and handed it to Ricky. He gave his hand a bit of a rub where it had been stung by the cold and pocketed the rest of his keys.

Both Ricky and Mr. Wilson watched Mrs. Wilson as her facial expression went from slack to startled. She looked as though she had just awakened from a nap. She shook her head, rubbed her eyes and looked around as though she wasn't sure where she was.

Ricky quickly pocketed the key and returned to her chores. She rushed through the work she usually did, made an excuse about having a lot of homework and left. As soon as she was out of sight of the farm, she ran all the way to the manor house.

Ben and Nick had given up calling for Alexa and

sat on the front porch waiting for Ricky. They saw her running in their direction and ran to meet her. She held the key up for them to see as she grew closer. All three of them cheered and hugged as Ricky handed the key to Ben. "We did it." They heard a cheerful voice beside them. "We got the key back and I learned what the Wilsons are doing with those poor dogs."

CHAPTER TWENTY-THREE

"Alexa!" Ben said. "We've been worried about you. Let's go to the house so you can tell us what happened."

They walked to the house barely saying a word. They all wanted to hear what Alexa had found out, but they also wanted the shelter of the house. They wanted Alexa to become visible, but not out in the open. When they reached the house Alexa appeared on the bottom step and walked up the stairs and into the house first. They all made themselves comfortable on the large stair case and turned to face Alexa.

Alexa's face was still pale and ghostly, though the other children were all flushed with fresh air and excitement. Alexa's eyes were bright and she looked ready to burst with her information. "I can't believe what I was able to do with Mrs. Wilson, can you Ricky?"

"I'm not really sure what happened there." Ricky said.

"I remembered hearing stories about people being possessed by ghosts when my mother and her friends were gossiping once. They didn't think I was listening, but I got so scared I couldn't sleep for days afterward. I had no idea that those stories would help me now a lifetime later! I wouldn't really say I possessed her though, so much as I just spoke for her for a moment." Alexa and Ricky went on to tell the boys what had just happened at the Wilson's farm. "When Ricky came over with the keys, I simply stepped into Mrs. Wilson's space and answered Mr. Wilson's question. He gave the key to Ricky and I stepped back out."

The boys commented on how impressed they were with what she had done and Ricky grew very quiet and withdrawn. After a few more moments of discussing what had occurred, Ricky asked, "Are the Wilsons stealing the dogs?"

Everyone became silent. They all realized the **repercussions** for both Ricky and Nick. Each was hoping for a different outcome concerning the Wilsons. "Yes Ricky," Alexa spoke gently, "it is the Wilsons. I followed Mr. Wilson around all day yesterday after he picked up the key. That big silver building with the loud fan is where they are keeping the dogs.

"Rufus is there, Nick. He is sad, but healthy. The

dogs are being taken care of but, they don't let them out of the cages. They feed them and give them shots of some medicine, but the poor things never get out to run around, or have fresh air. There are a lot of dogs in there. They have been taking dogs from other towns too. When they have a male and female of the same kind they intend to breed them and sell the puppies from..." she paused as if trying to remember, "from some kind of net. That part I didn't understand." she muttered.

Ricky and Nick looked confused, but Ben jumped in to explain. "The internet." he stated simply. Ricky and Nick nodded knowingly, but of course Alexa still looked confused. "It's hard to explain Alexa." Ben continued. "It's a new way of communicating between people; like writing letters or newspapers, only much more complex. It's a modern thing."

"Well it's not important that I understand, as long as the three of you do. They have that big fan on the building to drown out the noise the dogs make, but as they have been getting more dogs they have worried that the barking will get to be too much. That's the reason they've been building that new place in the woods. They have made it sound proof and they think that no one knows it's there. They are planning to move the dogs into the new building in the middle of the night on Friday."

"My poor Rufus." Nick moaned. "What are we going to do?"

K. E. SWANSON

"It's obvious." Alexa said. "You will simply have to go to the authorities."

The children discussed this idea for a while and came to the conclusion that it would be the simplest and most effective way to resolve the situation. They said goodbye to Alexa with a promise to return to fill her in on what happened as soon as possible.

They walked into town together and went straight to the police station. They walked up to the front desk and Nick asked to speak to a police detective. The woman at the desk glanced briefly over her shoulder, continued typing and said in a bored tone, "What is this concerning?"

"We know who's been stealing all the dogs around town!" Nick burst out.

"Oh, do you?" The secretary continued typing. "And you think it's a police matter do you?"

"Oh, yeah! You guys gotta throw these people in jail and get all the dogs back to their owners! We probably better get the humane society involved too..."

Ben nudged Nick and took over talking. "Actually we would like some advice as to how we can legally have our pets returned to us. We wouldn't want to cause any trouble by taking the matter into our own hands. Is there someone who has the time to talk to us?"

198

She sighed deeply, clicked her tongue and pushed her chair away from her desk. "I'll see if one of the **rookies** can take a few minutes to talk to you. Don't keep him too long though. The police are not here to settle squabbles between kids. You kids gotta learn to solve your own problems." The children heard her heals clicking down the hall, stop, and a moment later come back down the hall toward them again.

"**Constable** Brigoon will be with you in a moment." She said. "You just sit there quietly. I've got important work to do here."

A short time later a thick, muscular young man in a blue uniform came walking down the same hall. He stepped into the lobby and whispered, "You the kids that wanted to talk to a cop?"

They nodded and he motioned for them to follow him back down the hall. They entered a small room that was almost entirely filled up by a table surrounded by chairs. "Don't want to bother Miss Primell out there. She has more work to do than she has time for and she don't tolerate interruptions so good. Now what's the problem you kids got?"

Nick opened his mouth to speak, thought better of it and turned to Ben. "You've heard about all the dogs that have gone missing, I suppose?" Ben said.

Constable Brigoon nodded and Ben continued.

"We just found out who has them. It's Rodney and Jane Wilson. They've been stealing the dogs because they are going to breed them and sell them on the internet."

"I see." Constable Brigoon raised his eyebrows and scratched his head. "They been stealing dogs so they can start up a puppy mill. Who told you this? Where'd you get this information?"

None of the children spoke. No one knew what to say. They hadn't discussed how to answer this question and they obviously couldn't tell the constable that a ghost had told them. They all looked from the constable to one another until the silence became uncomfortable. Nick and Ben both began to speak at once and both stopped. Ben began again, "Our source wishes to remain **anonymous**. That's why we're here not her... or him. Our source didn't want to be involved ... um ...for ...a ... political reasons." Ben stumbled over his words and Ricky glared at him for the excuse he had come up with.

Constable Brigoon nodded slowly and thought for a few moments. "The Wilson's is good people you know. You don't want to be making no false **accusations** against good, hard working people. Let me go run this by my boss and I'll let you know." He got up and left the room.

"Political reasons?" Ricky whispered as she smacked the heal of her hand against her forehead. "I realize it must have been hard to come up with something off the top of your head, but political reasons?"

The constable returned to the room after a surprisingly short absence and shook his head. "The sarge says unless you got proof, there's no way we're running in there looking for no dogs. You can't just go making accusations against law abiding citizens when you got no proof. You got any proof? We actually don't even got any official reports filed about no missing dogs."

The children were disappointed, but had to admit that they had no proof. They left the police station and headed back to the manor house. Alexa greeted them at the door and was equally disappointed that the police refused to help. They sat down on the stairs again to brainstorm a new plan.

After over half an hour, many possibilities had been suggested, but they kept coming back to the fact that they needed to collect some evidence. Since Alexa was unable to pick anything up or move anything, it was obvious that the children would be at the forefront on this mission. They planned to set their alarm clocks and meet back at Mason Manor at midnight.

CHAPTER TWENTY-FOUR

Before he left his room, Ben had the forethought to leave a note for his grandparents telling them where he was going, who he was with and what they were doing. He walked across the roof outside his bedroom window in his sock feet and sat at the edge of the roof to put his running shoes on. His stomach was doing flip-flops as he climbed down to the ground; he felt uncomfortable going out in the middle of the night by himself and he knew that he and his friends were taking a big risk. The Wilson's were criminals, after all, and who knew what they would do to cover their tracks if they caught the children. Ben walked quickly to the forest path and, when he knew he was out of sight from his grandparents' house, he switched on his flashlight and began to run. He reached the Mason house at a quarter to twelve; fifteen minutes early. Ben had grown quite accustomed to the house, but was not used to being outside in the dark, so he decided he would be more comfortable waiting in the house for Ricky and Nick.

He walked up the front stairs and knocked on the door before walking in. He called out to Alexa. For a moment there was only silence, but then Ben was shocked to hear a loud wailing cry from up stairs. He called out to Alexa again, worried for his friend's well being. He looked to the top of the stairs and saw a **shimmery**, white figure. He knew instantly that it was not Alexa. The form was female, but was much taller than Alexa. She wore a long white dress that was in tatters at the bottom and at the sleeves. The figure was somewhat transparent; as Ben would have expected a ghost to look before he had met Alexa. She had long dark hair that was tangled and messy as though she had been sleeping on it for many days. Her face was white and her eye sockets were dark and empty. Ben shuddered and turned to run to the door, but once he had changed direction he found that the frightening figure was still in front of him only much closer.

"What have you done with her?" The ghost shrieked angrily.

Ben took a step back and the banshee advanced toward him. "I've done nothing. I don't know what you mean." Ben stammered. He stumbled and fell backward landing hard on the stairs.

The ghoul seemed to float closer and closer and

Ben attempted to scramble backward up the stairs without taking the time to get to his feet. It raised its arms up over its head and its face distorted in rage. Ben was sure it was about to fly at him and he screamed out for Alexa.

He heard a loud bang as the front door flew open and crashed against the wall behind. At the same moment Alexa materialized out of nowhere. To Ben's great relief, the apparition instantly vanished.

Nick, Ricky and Alexa ran to Ben, who lay on his back on the stairs, his face white and his eyes bulging. "What happened?" Ricky said.

"There was a ghost! It was about to attack me! It was horrible!" Ben voice **quavered** and his hands shook. "I don't know what it wanted. I've never seen anything so frightening in my whole life. It kept asking, what have you done with her?"

"Do you think it could have been Alexa's mother?" Nick looked around the room.

Ben looked to Alexa, not wanting to hurt her. "Yes, I think it might have been. I'm sorry Alexa, but it's the only thing that makes sense. It must have been you that she was asking about." Ben sat forward on the stairs and held his head in his hands. He ran his fingers through his hair and looked down at his friends. "That was so unexpected. I've never felt afraid in this house before."

"I don't know what to say Ben."Alexa said. "I feel terrible. I don't understand why I have never seen her before."

"It kind of makes sense." Nick said. "First of all, unless you are with us, you only seem to do things that were your routine when you were alive. I doubt that it was your routine to walk around the house in the middle of the night. The other thing is that if you were in the room with your mother's ghost, she wouldn't need to look for you, and that seems to be her whole purpose in being here."

"That all makes sense." Alexa agreed. "Do you really think that she would have hurt you if we hadn't shown up at that moment?"

"I certainly felt threatened. I don't really know what would have happened. Thank goodness you guys all got here when you did."

"I guess you don't feel up to going to the Wilson's to look for evidence now, do you?" Nick said.

"Actually, the last thing I feel like doing right now is going home to be alone all night. There's no way I would be able to fall asleep after what just happened. We might as well go ahead with our plans. Otherwise we would all just have to sneak out again tomorrow night."

"And tomorrow night is the last night before they move the dogs. We wouldn't be smart to leave it to the last night." Ricky added. "So, let's go."

The children approached the Wilson's farm silently and crept up to the silver building that housed the dogs. Alexa volunteered to be on watch for Mr. and Mrs. Wilson, though she wasn't able to move too far from the key that hung around Ben's neck. The children walked around the building looking for any doors that might have been left unlocked or windows that they could look into. They had no success, but Nick suggested in a hushed voice that they should look one more time and that they should focus higher on the building. Half way around Ricky stopped them and pointed up. Below the gable end of the roof was a vent. The children were uncertain what good it would do them; however, it was the only opening to the building that they had discovered. Ricky whispered that she knew where they could find a ladder and went to retrieve it. In the meantime Ben discussed an idea with Nick and Alexa.

When Ricky returned with the ladder, they took a moment to fill her in on the plan and then Ben positioned the ladder under the vent and began to climb. When he reached the top, he reached inside the collar of his jacket and pulled the key out of his shirt. He removed the cord from around his neck and wrapped it around his hand. He examined the vent closely and then held the key in the fingers of his right hand. He fed the tip of the key through the vent hole and pushed it sideways through the vent. He dangled the key through the vent for a few minutes then pulled on the cord. He had difficulty extracting the key. It got stuck and he had to use his pocket knife to pry up the slats on the vent to get it out. When he finally got it loose, he climbed down from the ladder and met the children at the bottom. Alexa materialized as Ben reached the ground.

"Were you able to see inside?" Ben asked.

"Yes." She whispered. "There seems to be a small hatch at the opposite end of the building under that big fan, but it's up high. I don't know if it will do you any good, but let's go around the building and have a look."

They took the ladder and moved around to the other side of the building. They leaned the ladder up to the building and Ben climbed up to the top of the building again. He pried open the hatch, but was unable to get high enough to look through the opening. "Alexa," he whispered, "I'm going to dangle the key through the opening again. Can you go in and see if it is worth taking a picture from there. We need to have something to bring back to use as proof.

"Yes I'll go in. Go ahead and put the key in."

Once again, Ben removed the cord from around his neck and reached up to try to put the key through the hole. An electrical cord was dangling beside his hand and he brushed it aside and dangled the key through the opening. Just as the key went into the opening the big noisy fan stopped. The sudden absence of the noise was startling, but the silence didn't last long. The dogs, who had also been surprised by the quietness, resumed barking, only now, without the fan to drown out the noise, it was quite loud.

Ben saw a light come on inside the Wilson's house and panicked. He knew he wouldn't have long to hide before Mr. Wilson came out to check on the dogs. In his rush to get down the ladder he let go of the cord that held the key. Ben's heart sank. He knew instantly that the key was lost to him. There was no way into the locked building. Between the fear and the disappointment, he felt like he was going to be sick. He was still aware that he needed to rush to hide, if he was going to keep himself safe, so he scrambled down the ladder and ran with his two friends to the woods.

Mr. Wilson walked out his front door and went over to the dog building. He yawned, rubbed his eyes then climbed the ladder and reconnected the cord Ben had knocked loose. The fan started up and Mr. Wilson plodded back into the house.

"I guess he was too tired to realize that he hadn't left the ladder there." Ricky reasoned. "Hopefully he won't realize tomorrow either. Where is Alexa, Ben?"

Ricky noticed the forlorn look on Ben's face even in the moonlight and she said, "Oh no, what happened?"

"I dropped the key." Ben held his hands to his temples and shook his head. "Now I don't know how we'll ever get it back."

"We'll just have to go back tomorrow night and take pictures inside that building and hope that it will be enough proof for the police. Then we'll have to try to be there when they go bust the Wilsons. That way one of us can try to sneak in and find the key." Nick said.

The children all knew that it was a long shot that they would be able to recover the key that way, but a slight chance was better than no chance at all, so they took some **consolation** in Nick's idea.

CHAPTER TWENTY-FIVE

Ben walked up the school steps Thursday morning with dark circles under his eyes and a rooster's tail in his hair. He leaned against the railing and waited for the bell to ring. He scanned the school yard for Nick and saw his friend just getting out of a slightly dented small yellow car. As the car pulled away from the curb Nick unrolled the top of a fast food bag and pulled out a breakfast burger. Ben saw Nick look around the yard until their eyes met and Nick trudged over to meet him.

"Did you get enough sleep? I don't know if I could have slept if it had been me that Mrs. Mason was after. Either way it was a pretty short night. I don't know how I'll stay awake today." Nick rambled on and on, but Ben didn't have the energy to stop him.

When the bell rang the two boys trudged into the school and sat at their desks. Mr. Weir handed out a surprise test and the class gave a collective groan. Ben felt he would have done fine if he had had a good night's sleep, but struggled to focus enough to do well on the test.

Half an hour into the morning, the classroom door silently opened and someone quietly shuffled around at the back of the room. A few students turned to look which caught Ben attention. He turned to the back of the room and caught Ricky's eye just as Mr. Weir spoke. "Ricky, this is your third time late this week. Come here and talk to me."

Ricky approached Mr. Weir's desk apprehensively, spoke to the teacher in hushed tones, then walked to the back of the room and out the classroom door. She returned fifteen minutes later with a pink slip of paper in her hand and slouched heavily into her seat.

At break time the three friends met outside with their lunches. Ben began eating a sandwich as Nick pulled a giant chocolate muffin out of the same fast food bag that his breakfast had come from. Ricky had nothing.

The boys shared portions of their lunches with her and Nick **tactlessly** asked, "Did your mom go on strike or something?"

Ricky blushed and stumbled over her words trying to respond. "She – um – she's – well. I guess she's out of money right now, or she's too busy to go to the grocery store or something. She hasn't bought groceries in a couple of weeks and there's nothing at all left to eat at our house."

"You can eat at my house tonight, and I'm sure Gran will pack you some food to take home. Don't worry Ricky, things will get better." Ben said.

"I've got a detention after school too. Mr. Weir is sending me to the school counsellor because I've been late too many times." Ricky rubbed the tension that was building in the back of her neck and sighed heavily.

That evening, Ben went to bed quite early after seeing Ricky off with a big bag of food. They had talked quietly of their plans to meet again at the Mason house at midnight. Ben had tried to phone his father and for the tenth night in a row had no answer. The voice mail was full, so Ben did not leave a message. The last thing he did before falling asleep was to reset his alarm clock for eleven thirty.

Ben approached the house, early again, with the intention of waiting outside until the other children showed up. When he got close enough he recognized the familiar form of Alexa pressed closely to the side of the house out on the front porch. He ran up and whispered a greeting to his friend.

"Ben, I'm so glad you're here! There is a man in

the house. I'm frightened of him and I'm afraid my mother will show up again. What should we do?"

"Do you recognize the man?" Ben said.

"I've never seen him before. He's tall with an average build; middle aged. He has short dark hair." She paused to try to remember more. "He seems very sad. I thought I might have heard him weeping."

The description was of little help; it described half of the men Ben knew. He motioned for Alexa to follow and crept up to a window to peek in. He could barely see the man through the darkness, sitting on the stairs holding his head in his hands. Ben was shocked at how it brought him back to last night when he had sat in the exact same spot, in the exact same position. He watched the man a few moments more and the longer he looked the more familiar the man seemed. Ben furrowed his brow, squinted his eyes and moved his head slightly lower to try to get a better look. Ben was staring so intently at the man, he almost didn't notice when the man looked up and stared directly at the window where he and Alexa stood.

Ben recognized him right away. He turned to Alexa and said, "It's my dad! We can't let him see you, but can you still come in with me?"

Alexa nodded and faded quickly from sight. Ben ran to the door and went in, not bothering to close the door behind him. "Dad!" he yelled and ran into his father's open arms.

Still clinging tightly to his son, Ben's father asked incredulously, "It's so good to see you, but what are you doing here this time of night?"

"It's a long story Dad. What are you doing here? Why didn't you come to the house? Gran and Grandpa are starting to get worried about you."

Ben's father sighed. "I had to see you, Ben. I have to go away for a while, but there are some things I have to explain to you first. This isn't going to be easy for you to hear. Let's sit down."

They moved to the chairs by the fire place and sat down. Ben shuffled around in the chair trying to find a comfortable position then settled stiffly into place and his father began to speak. "This is so hard for me to tell you Ben, but... your mother didn't die of an illness like I've been telling you. They say she was murdered and now ... now they're accusing me." His father waited while this information sunk in.

"That's ridiculous!" Ben said. "Anyone who has seen you and Mom together can tell you love each other! Anyone can see you could never kill her!'

"You and I know that, Ben; and every one of our friends believes me. It's the police I have to convince of that. When I moved you here, they had just told me that I

215

was a suspect. I figured it was only a matter of time before I was cleared, so I sent you here to protect you until I was no longer a suspect. Unfortunately I haven't been cleared yet. As a matter of fact, now there are no suspects other than me. I could see that they were going to arrest me soon, so I ran. I don't want to break the law, but if I'm sitting in a jail somewhere, there's no way for me to find out who really did kill your mother."

A tear ran down Ben's cheek as the full **implication** of what his father had said hit him. His mother was murdered. Someone had **intentionally** taken the life of his kind, sweet mother. Not only had he lost his mother, now he was on the verge of losing his father too. His father was about to go into hiding for, who knows how long, and eventually there was a possibility that his father would go to jail for a very long time. Ben bent over in his seat, held his head in his hands and cried.

Ben talked to his father a while longer and then, afraid of needing to explain why his friends were showing up, he made an excuse about having to get home to bed. He made his father promise to stay to see him again the next day, gave him a long hug and said goodbye.

"By the way, Ben," His father asked, "who was that girl that I saw standing at the window with you?"

"You saw her?"

"Do you have a girlfriend? Is that why you are

coming to this house in the middle of the night?" His father smiled.

"No. Dad, she's just a friend. Her parents aren't around much and she doesn't have much to eat at her house, so I was bringing her some food. Gran doesn't mind." He borrowed Ricky's story to explain Alexa. Under the circumstances there was little chance he would get caught in a lie.

When Ben walked outside, he looked toward the path where he would expect both Nick and Ricky to approach from. He saw the glow of a flashlight and walked over to his friends. Alexa appeared too. Ben looked at them questioningly.

"I could see that you and your father would be having a lengthy conversation and I wanted to give you privacy. I didn't know how to let you know I was leaving without making your father suspicious. Plus I didn't want Nick and Ricky to interrupt you and your father, so I met them on the porch and they came back here. Is everything alright? You look very upset."

"I am very upset, but we don't have time to talk about it right now. I'll tell you guys what's going on with my dad tomorrow. Right now, let's do what we came here for. Let's go to the Wilson's."

The three children started to walk away and Alexa stopped them. "I won't be able to go with you. You don't have the key with you. I will go to the building and wait where the key is, in case there is any way I can help. You likely won't see me there tonight, but I'll be there."

"That's right. I completely forgot that you wouldn't be able to stay with me when I don't have the key." Ben smacked his palm against his forehead. "Thanks for your support. We'll be glad to know you're in there if we need you."

The children walked to the Wilson's in silence. When they arrived, the ladder was where they had left it the day before. Nick pulled his father's compact digital camera out of his pocket and handed it to Ben. Ricky stood watch at the end of the building that was closer to the house and Nick stood near the doors to the dog building. Ben climbed the ladder. When Ben's hands reached the top of the ladder he was still too low to be able to reach up with the camera to take pictures in the building. Although he felt very unstable, he reached up and grasped the edge of the hatch opening with his empty hand. He continued to climb up the ladder until his feet were on the rung that was third from the top.

He held the camera up to the opening and took a picture. He couldn't see what he was taking a picture of so he had to bring the camera down to his eyes and look at the image he had captured. There was nothing recognizable in the photo that could be taken to the police as evidence, so Ben reached up and, holding the camera at a different angle, took another picture. He checked the image again and reached up to take another picture. He continued to do this for five or six more pictures, when he suddenly heard Ricky's voice below him whispering urgently.

"The lights went on in the house. I think he must have seen the camera flashing! We have to get out of here! Wait; he's coming Ben! You don't have time to get down. Stay there and be quiet! I'll hide in the bush."

Ben watched Ricky run into the woods. He could hear little over the sound of the fan and his drumming heart. He tried to climb down a couple of rungs on the ladder to a more stable position, but the ladder rattled in time with his knocking knees. He could see Mr. Wilson coming around the corner of the building. He wrapped the cord of the camera around his wrist and grasped the edge of the hatch opening with both hands. He began to look around for Nick. He hadn't seen his friend run into the woods and Ben feared Nick would get caught. Finally he spotted Nick crouched down behind a rain barrel that was positioned right beside the door of the dog building.

Mr. Wilson unlocked the doors of the dog building, turned on a flashlight and walked in. Ben almost fell off the ladder with shock when he saw Nick follow Mr. Wilson into the building. This had not been a part of their plan.

Nick hadn't had time to run to the forest to hide when he saw Ricky go by. He crouched down behind the barrel and almost decided to run to the woods when Mr. Wilson entered the building. Nick suddenly thought to himself that this could be his only opportunity to get into this building. He had the chance to save both his dog and Alexa's key at the same time so he ran into the building without thinking; before he had a chance to consider the consequences.

Inside, he hid under a table in the corner and watched Mr. Wilson look around with his flashlight. He crept out from under the table when Mr. Wilson had wandered to the far side of the building. He wanted to go to where the hatch was that Ben had been looking through and search for the key below it. On his way to the spot below the hatch, Nick had to pass a few dog kennels. The dogs barked at him as he passed, which wasn't noticeable to Mr. Wilson in the ruckus that the large number of dogs made in the building. Ben thought one of the barks sounded familiar. He looked over his shoulder to see the face of his beloved pet staring through the bars of a cage. He couldn't resist. He felt compelled to reach over and open the latch on the cage. He had just opened the latch when he saw Mr. Wilson coming back in his direction. Nick made a dash for the door, but Mr. Wilson grabbed him by the scruff of the neck.

By this time Ben had climbed down from the ladder. He was just peeking in the doors of the building when he saw, by the light of Mr. Wilson's flashlight, that he had Nick by the back of his shirt. Ben began to search around for something that he could use to try to help him to free his friend. He had no idea what he was going to do with it, but his hand closed around the handle of a straw broom. He picked it up and was about to charge into the building when he saw something strange.

Behind Nick and Mr. Wilson, Ben could see Rufus sitting in a cage. Rufus's body gave a sudden violent twitch and after a brief pause he gave a great shudder. The dog then butted its head against the cage door and it popped open. Oddly, Rufus stumbled from his cage. Ben had never seen an animal look so unsure of its footing, he wondered if the dog could have been drugged. Ben was also surprised to hear that the dog's growl sounded rather strangely like 'grrrr' and its bark actually sounded like the words 'bark, bark'. The dog lunged at the man who was attacking its master. Rufus bared his teeth, jumped at Mr. Wilson and grabbed onto the arm that held Nick. Rufus shook the arm until Mr. Wilson gave in to the pain and let go of Nick to try to shake the dog off his arm.

Once Nick was loose from the man's grasp, he turned to the door and ran. Ben joined him and the two boys headed for the forest path. They found Ricky waiting for them on the path and the three children ran toward the manor house. When they got to the house, they crouched down behind some shrubs and waited to see if Mr. Wilson was following them.

A few moments after they got into their hiding places, they heard the sound of someone crashing through the woods. They were all astounded to see Rufus come stumbling out of the brush. He lumbered along, tripped over his own front feet, stumbled to the ground and landed on his face. He then sat on his hind quarters for a moment and frantically began to scratch himself all over. Rufus stood back up, began running, and again, tripped on his front feet. This time, because he had more momentum, when Rufus fell, he did a full somersault before lunging forward, flying through the air and landing on the ground in front of the children. He stood back up and spit something out of his mouth at Ben's feet. Rufus's body then convulsed briefly, became very stiff and collapsed to the ground.

Nick jumped forward and wrapped his arms around his dog crying, "Don't die Rufus. I just got you back. Don't die!"

Rufus wiggled around a little, squirmed out of Nicks grasp and sat up in front of Nick. He panted a few times, gave a little bark and licked Nicks face happily.

Just then, Alexa stepped forward from the darkness. She smoothed her dress down with her hands and then reached up to fuss with her hair. When she seemed to think she was all straightened out she stepped towards Ben, bent down and picked something up from the ground.

Ben stared, open mouthed at Alexa. Not only was he surprised that she was holding something, he was surprised that she was holding the key. "You moved something Alexa!" he whispered in the darkness.

Alexa looked down at her hand and just as the surprise registered on her face, the key fell to the ground. Ben reached to the ground and picked it up. "Do you still trust me to hang onto this for you?" he asked Alexa. "And what just happened there?"

Alexa wrinkled her nose at Rufus and began to explain. "I saw an opportunity to help, but I had no idea how unpleasant it would be. After Nick unlocked Rufus's cage, I wondered if I could jump into his body the way I had with Mrs. Wilson. I gave it a try, but I won't be doing that again anytime soon. It was so uncomfortable and awkward! The moment I was in him, I was tortured by a horrible itchyness. I just wanted to scratch myself all over; and do you have any idea how difficult it is to coordinate running on four feet? Anyway, I bit Mr. Wilson and held on until Nick had a chance to get away. Then I grabbed the key and ran off. I am quite surprised that Mr. Wilson didn't give chase. I wonder what he could be doing."

"Maybe we better go back and check." Ricky spoke up.

"I need to do something with Rufus first." Nick dug in his backpack and pulled out a piece of rope. "I need to tie him up somewhere. I don't want to lose him again."

"I know the perfect spot to hide him." Ben said. "Follow me."

Ben walked over to the overgrown willow tree in the manor house's front yard. He parted the branches and disappeared into the foliage. Nick and Ricky followed and found themselves in a hollow beneath the branches of the tree. Ricky shone her flashlight around the tunnel under the tree. "I wonder what this is for." She indicated a spot where an unusual symbol was carved into the trunk of the tree.

"Who knows?" Nick searched the ground and found a root that looped up from the soil. He tied Rufus's rope to the root, hugged his dog and said, "I'll be back for you soon, boy. Be good."

CHAPTER TWENTY-SIX

The group snuck through the forest, back to the Wilson's farm. They arrived to find that Mr. Wilson had gone back into the house to rouse Mrs. Wilson and the two of them were frantically loading dogs and dog crates into their van. When the van was filled to capacity they both got in and drove off toward the new building that was hidden in the woods.

Ben turned to the others and said, "He must have recognized you Nick. I think they are trying to move everything to the new building. They probably think that you will go to the police in the morning. They must assume that you don't know about the new building, so they are going to move all the evidence there tonight."

Nick nodded and said, "So that if the police come here in the morning there will be no proof of their crime. What are we going to do?"

"That's easy," Ricky said "we go to the police now. Did you get any good pictures Ben?"

Ben pulled the camera from his pocket and they gathered around to look at the photos on the digital display. A couple were too blurry, but it was clear, in a few photos, that the Wilson's had a building filled with dogs locked into kennels.

"We should probably go back through the clearing with the new dog building in it just to make sure that's where they are going. If we brought the police back here and the dogs and the Wilsons weren't there, they would never take us seriously." Ben suggested. Everyone agreed and the group headed off to the clearing.

When they neared the area Ben whispered to the others. "I know a place we can watch them from, but we won't be seen." He hedged along the clearing, hidden by the darkness and his friends followed closely behind. They came to the **derelict** building he had spotted on the far side of the clearing the first day he had found the building site and crouched down beside it. The children were able to watch the Wilson's, who were moving dogs and other items into the new building by the light of the van headlights. They watched for a few minutes and felt satisfied that this would be where they would bring the police."Let's get going." Ben whispered and they all began to move.

There was suddenly a loud cracking sound and

Ricky, who had been in the lead, vanished from sight. A moment later the remaining children heard a **blood-curdling** scream from somewhere just in front of them.

Ben and Nick looked at one another with both eyes and mouths agape. They looked ahead and, by the pale light of the moon, could just barely make out a dark hole in boards that were covering the ground. "Hold onto my feet." Ben commanded Nick. The two boys moved to look into the hole, but the boards were too rotten. Ben jumped back when he felt the boards giving way beneath him.

"Are you insane?" They heard Alexa whisper behind them. "Why would you risk getting injured when I can easily go down into that hole to check on Ricky?"

"That's a good point." Ben said and both boys scuffled away from the hole in the ground. Alexa disappeared from sight and a moment later they could hear Alexa and Ricky talking.

In the hole Alexa found Ricky huddled on the floor at the edge of a small underground space. Ricky was cradling one arm with the other. "Are you okay Ricky?" Alexa asked. "You've hurt your arm. Is that why you screamed?"

"No. Look over there." Ricky pointed to the far side of the gloomy hole.

There, in a beam of moonlight, Alexa could see

some moth eaten fabric and some white objects that almost appeared to glow in the moonlight. She moved closer and gasped as she recognized what the objects were. They were human bones. Alexa looked down and studied the skeleton. It was clothed in a pale pink dress that would have been quite fancy if it was still intact. The feet were wearing black patent leather shoes. The skull was resting on a bed of long dark hair. Alexa reached up as if to touch her own long dark hair. She sighed and sat on the floor beside the skeleton.

"What's going on? Are you guys okay down there?" Nick whispered from above.

"I'm hurt. I think my arm is broken." Ricky's voice was shaky. "We must be in the cellar of this building. There is a skeleton down here. I think it must be Alexa's body. She seems to be in a kind of **trance**."

"I think the Wilson's heard you scream! They are coming this way!" Ben whispered urgently. "I'm going to throw the key down to you so that Alex can stay with you. We need to run or we're going to get caught. Stay quiet; we'll come back with help as soon as we can!"

Ricky heard the key land with a soft thud on the dirt floor of the cellar and then she heard Ben and Nick's footsteps running off. She heard Mr. Wilson's voice yelling at them to stop and then threatening to get them.

Ben instinctually ran in the direction of Mason

Manor. He knew he could find a place to hide there, but forgot momentarily that his father was hiding there too. When the two boys ran up the front steps and burst through the front door, they were startled to see Ben's father looking just as startled to see them. "Dad, hide; there's someone coming!"

Ben's father darted into a nearby room and Ben and Nick turned just in time to see Mr. Wilson burst through the front door. He stopped short, looked around and focused on the two boys standing at the base of the stairs.

Ben froze in his panic and stared at Mr. Wilson. As he watched, he noticed Mr. Wilson's focus shift from himself and Nick to something at the top of the stairs. Ben turned around and saw the terrifying ghostly image of Mrs. Mason standing at the top of the stairs. The image grew more clear and almost seemed to glow in the darkness. The dress was torn and ragged and the eye sockets were hollow and black. The banshee raised its hand and pointed at Mr. Wilson. "What have you done?" Its voice was low and horse. "Where is she?" The voice grew louder. "What have you done with her?" The demon shrieked.

It raised its arms in the air and seemed to dive from the top of the stair case. The glowing form swooped down, over the heads of the boys, toward Mr. Wilson. The terrified man turned and ran back out the front door. The horrible image of the ghost seemed to vanish the moment Mr. Wilson crossed the **threshold** of the house. The boys heard him stumble down the stairs and run off into the forest.

Ben and Nick were just as breathless from the scene they had witnessed as they were from the run to the manor house. They stood catching their breath as Ben's father peeked out from the room he had hidden in.

"What on earth is going on here? Who was chasing you two and what are you doing out at this time of night?"

Ben explained to his father about the dognapping that had been going on around town. He told his father about Rufus and how the three children had gone to the police for help and been turned away. He explained that they had gone to find proof of the crime and that Mr. Wilson had seen them and chased them to the manor house.

"You kids have gotten in over your heads here. I'm going to call Gran and Grandpa on my cell phone and tell them what has happened. You two should both go home. I'm going to have to get out of here after I call; this house won't be a safe place for me to hide anymore with the police investigating a crime so close." Ben's father reached into his pocket for his phone, but Ben stopped him.

"I can't go home yet dad. Our friend Ricky is hurt

and she's trapped in an old cellar near the place they are moving the dogs to. We need to get help and go back for her."

"Okay." His father sighed. "I'll call and tell your grandfather to let the police know that they will need to rescue your friend. I can understand that you will want to be there when she comes out of the cellar." He paused as though he had just thought of something. "What scared away the guy that was chasing you?"

"A big barn owl flew down the stairs at him. I suppose he must have thought it was a ghost." Ben forced a little chuckle. "I guess it's things like that that make people think this place is haunted."

A half hour later, after Ben had said goodbye to his father, the two boys walked back down the forest path to the Wilson's farm. Before they even came around the side of the barn, they could see the flashing red and blue lights of the police cars that had convened on the property. Ben and Nick walked straight to Constable Brigoon and told him about Ricky being trapped in the cellar on the adjacent property. The constable and a couple of other police officers took the ladder and some rope from the barn and followed Ben and Nick to the dilapidated building.

As they walked close to the hole into the cellar Ben called out to Ricky. "We're back Ricky are you okay?"

"No, I'm in pain. What took you guys so long? It's really creepy being down here with this skeleton."

"Skeleton?" Constable Brigoon said.

A short time later Constable Brigoon was assisting Ricky to get into an ambulance and the police investigation had spilled over from the farm to the cellar and to the new building. The boys heard a few cops talking about the identity of the remains in the cellar. Ben stepped forward to offer an explanation.

"I think it might be Alexa Mason. We've been researching the Mason Manor for a while now and we found out that the daughter of the Mason's went missing. I guess they never figured out what happened to her. They never found a body."

EPILOGUE

A few weeks later, Ricky's arm was in a cast and the Wilson's were in jail awaiting their trial. Ben's father was deep in hiding, but the papers across the country were carrying the story of the murder and the disappearance of the primary suspect. The stolen dogs had all been returned to their rightful owners and Alexa's body had been **exhumed** from the cellar grave.

The **coroner** determined that Alexa had died of a broken neck. With the skeleton being the only remains it was difficult to determine much more about the details of Alexa's death, but he did detect some **trauma** to her skull as well as the injury to her spinal cord, so he determined that she may have fallen to her death. The fact that the body was hidden, led the coroner to conclude that Alexa had been murdered.

Ben had **campaigned** for a proper burial and a small

funeral for Alexa. The town council, a local church and Ben's grandparents agreed to foot the bill for the burial.

Ben and his friends spent a lot of time with Alexa leading up to the burial. They knew that they would be saying their final goodbyes to their friend.

On the day of the funeral the three children walked **solemnly** to the manor house. They walked up the stairs, knocked on the door and walked into the house. Alexa was there waiting for them.

"Why the sad faces?" she said. "It's not like I'm dying today. That happened a long time ago. We are just completing the process. I'm sad to be leaving you three too, but it will be a relief to put an end to this repetitive existence. Besides, maybe this is the closure that my mother needs."

Ben touched the key that was hanging on top of his sweater. "Would you like me to put the key into your coffin to be buried with you?" he said.

"Goodness no!" Alexa looked startled by the idea of it. "It would be terrible to have it locked away again. I would much rather you kept it, Ben. Keep it as a reminder of our friendship; besides maybe you could continue to search the house for what it opens. Just promise me that you will never stuff it into a box under your bed." She laughed.

Ben snickered too and said, "I promise you,

Alexa, that if I ever take it off I'll put it on a window sill or hang it on the wall or something."

"Hey, I found out why Miss Crumbey was buying dog food that day." Nick slurped and tucked a wad of candy into his cheek before continuing. "Mrs. Thompson was shopping in my mom's store and she told her that she has a new dog. It turns out Miss Crumbey found a little dog hiding in her garden. It had a lot of cuts and bruises and it was shaking like a leaf. She took it in to nurse it back to health. Once it was a bit better, it started causing too much trouble with the cats and she had to give it away so she gave it to Mrs. Thompson."

"I wonder if it was the dog that George's gang was stoning. It would be good to know it survived." Ben said.

After a short visit and a few tears the children said goodbye to their spectral friend. Ben once again felt the awkwardness of wanting to touch Alexa, but not being able to. He longed to embrace her, put a comforting hand on her shoulder or give her a hug goodbye. Instead he said what words he could, looked down at the floor and shuffled his feet around a little.

They said goodbye and walked to the door. Ben took one last glance over his shoulder at his friend. She stood on the grand stair case wearing a slight smile of fondness for her friends and faded until she had disappeared completely.

Later that morning the three children were dressed in their nicest clothing. They met at the little church that was closest to the Mason manor and sat in the pew usually reserved for family. Ben's grandparents sat in the pew behind the children.

The pastor gave a short sermon and commented on the tragedy of a life cut short. He also spoke about the trauma of her family's having lost her and never having had the closure of a funeral until now. He prayed that the ceremony they were conducting would give them some peace at last.

After the funeral the group went out to the church yard for the burial. The small casket was lowered into the hole in the ground. Ben saw a flash of white out of the corner of his eye and wondered whether it had been Alexa or her mother who had attended the funeral.

Ben spent the next few days trying to keep himself busy. He spent time with Nick and Ricky, but the group didn't feel the same without the fourth friend. All three of the children were glum and talked about little, but Alexa.

Ben felt that he needed to privately say goodbye to Alexa in order to have closure for himself. He used his allowance to buy a small bouquet of flowers and walked over to the church cemetery.

At the church, Ben walked to the mound of fresh soil that was Alexa's grave. He knelt down in front of it and studied the small headstone that his grandparents had purchased for the grave. It included a small statue of an angel, which Ben was pleased looked a little bit like Alexa. He laid the flowers at the headstone and whispered, "I miss you my friend."

"Yes," a voice from behind him spoke. "It has been a little dull around here since the mystery of the missing dogs was solved, hasn't it?"

Ben turned to look behind him for the person who spoke, but there was no one there. When he turned back to the grave, Ben was astonished to see Alexa poised as though she was leaning on her own headstone.

"What! Where did you come from? I thought..." Ben muttered, not knowing exactly what to say next. "I'm so happy to see you though. Wait till we tell Nick and Ricky! We've all missed you so much!" Ben paused for a moment. "I'm sorry Alexa. I'm being **insensitive**, because I'm so happy to see you. Is everything alright? Why are you still here? How do you feel about not having... gone on to ..."

"Don't worry so much, Ben. I'm happy to see you too. I haven't talked to you in a while because I'm not really sure how to do this passing on thing. At first I thought it would just happen. When nothing happened I thought that maybe I just wasn't trying hard enough. The trouble is I don't really know how to try harder. That's why I'm here. I thought that if I came to my grave, I might be able to... you know."

"Let's think about this for a minute here. I would have thought that it would just happen too. It shouldn't take an effort to pass on, should it? It should just happen." Ben paused, deep in thought. "Maybe, the location of your body was just a piece of the puzzle. Maybe we need to find out how you died, or who killed you, or what the key unlocks." Ben smiled widely at his **phantom** friend. "Maybe we have another mystery to solve together!"

GLOSSARY

Page 1

plummet - to drop steeply and suddenly downward

exertion - an act that involves great effort

audible - loud enough to be heard

pursuers - someone who follows in order to capture someone

betrayal - to be disloyal to

Page 2

eternity - a very long, seemingly endless period of time

confinement - a period of time during which one is restricted to a specific space

Page 3

rotate - to turn around a fixed point

vertical - in an upright position

orient - to get used to a certain situation

belligerent - ready to start a fight

righteousness - pride that comes from having been right

Page 4

self-assurance - confidence in self

agape - with mouth wide open

Page 6

casual - done without thought or planning

retrieved - to pick up something

ornate - greatly decorated

Page 7

predicament - a bad situation

Page 8

resident - to live in a place for a long term

embankment - a raised area of earth

satisfactory - good enough

Page 9

ambush - an unexpected attack

seized - to take

Page 10

ensued - to begin soon after

bewildered - confused

Page 11

furrowed - wrinkled

Page 14

Tom Sawyer - a character from the Mark Twain novel of the same name, who is very adventurous

Page 15

gestured - pointed

depression - a feeling of sadness

all terrain quad - four wheeled motorized bike for use in rugged areas

contrast - things that are greatly different

Page 16

tentative - slow and careful

overwhelming - having an emotionally powerful effect

Page 17

benevolent - kind or showing goodwill

Page 18

domain - an area owned or controlled by a particular person

gable - the triangular top section on the side wall of a house

Page 20

distracted - showing a lack of concentration

Page 21

geode - a hollow rock filled with crystals on the inside

Page 22

amethyst - a purple, crystallized stone that is a variety of quartz

mica - a shiny silver mineral deposit on a rock

compartment - an area of enclosed space

Page 23

nausea - a feeling of sickness in the stomach

compelled - to make something happen by force

Page 27

absence - something not being there

Page 28

dishevelled - looking messy

Page 30

custodians - somebody responsible for looking after property. Staff members who clean the school at the end of the day.

Page 34

condolences - an expression of sympathy to someone who is grieving a death

Page 38

incredulously – unable or unwilling to believe something

ingenious - clever, original and effective

Page 40

descendants - a person, animal or plant related to one that lived in the past

foliage - the leaves of a plant or tree

resided - to live in a particular place

Page 41

grandeur - to be grand or very impressive

foyer - the entrance hall in a house or building

tapestries - a heavy piece of fabric with a woven pattern or picture, used as a wall hanging

accumulated - to collect

occupied - lived in

Page 42

disintegrating - to break into small pieces

scrutiny - close, careful, and thorough examination

vaguely – unclear

Page 43

disembodied - coming from somebody who cannot be seen in a way that may be eerie or frightening

implored - to plead with somebody to do something

Page 45

shiner - black eye

Page 46

obstruction - an act of blocking somebody or something

cronies - a close friend, especially one of long standing

Page 47

interrogation - the act of questioning somebody carefully and aggressively

confirmation - proof that something is right or true

Page 48

triumphant - displaying or feeling great pride in having achieved a victory

Page 49

sheepish - showing embarrassment as a result of having done something awkward or wrong

destination - the place to which somebody or something is going or must go

ruckus - a noisy and unpleasant disturbance

sidled - to move up to something in a casual manor

Page 50

foreclose - when the bank takes back a property with a mortgage because the payments have not been made

naturopathy - a type of medicine based on the belief that diet, mental state, exercise, breathing, and other natural factors are important to the origin and treatment of disease

Page 51

non-confrontational - not challenging or hostile

Page 52

poncho - a simple outer garment for the upper body in the form of a single piece of heavy cloth, often wool, with a slit in it for the head

noxious - very unpleasant

Page 56

dominated - to be the most clearly visible thing in the room

Page 57

tentatively - done in a slow careful way

lustre - shine

threadbare - so heavily used that the soft part of the fabric has been worn away to reveal the threads beneath

Page 58

deteriorated - worn out

revealing - giving new, valuable information

Page 60

response - an answer

ill intentions - something bad that someone plans to do

Page 63

reassurance - the act of making somebody feel less anxious or worried

awkward - shy, uncomfortable, and embarrassed

promptness - arriving on time

Page 64

sarcasm - remarks that mean the opposite of what they seem to say and are intended to mock or put down

dunce - somebody who is regarded as slow to learn or as generally unintelligent

Page 65

fungus - a growth on a plant that can include mildew, mold or mushrooms

satisfying - to make somebody feel pleased or content

accomplish - to complete something successfully

Page 66

intrusion - an interruption of somebody's peace or privacy

Page 67

veered - to suddenly change direction

déjà vu - a feeling of having already experienced the moment at another time

hesitantly - slow to do or say something because of indecision or lack of confidence

profusely - happening in large amounts

retreat - a movement away from danger or a confrontation

Page 68

edible - something that is meant to be eaten

torture - to inflict extreme pain or physical punishment on somebody

Page 69

intuition - a special power to understand

Page 72

ornate - having a lot of decoration

elaborately - made with a lot of intricate detail or decoration

transferred - to move from one place to another

Page 76

interject - to say something in a way that interrupts

Page 82

unfounded - not clearly true

ashen - extremely pale in appearance

Page 83

emphatically - said with great definiteness

dumbfounded - to make somebody temporarily speechless with astonishment

jutted - to stick out

Page 86

indulgent - tending to be tolerant and generally allowing people to have what they want

Page 87

tactics - the art of creating and implementing a plan

culminate - to come or bring something to an end, especially an exciting end

Page 88

cavalier - showing an arrogant or jaunty disregard or lack of respect for something or somebody

Page 89

reprimand - to scold for having done something wrong

Page 93

fictitious - invented by somebody's imagination

Page 95

foliage - the leaves of a plant or tree

Page 97

incense - a substance, usually fragrant gum or wood, that gives off a pleasant smell when burned

Page 99

unconscientiously - without thought

Page 100

disheveled - a messy look to hair or clothing

Page 101

pugnacious - inclined to fight or be aggressive

Page 107

adrenaline - a hormone secreted during periods excitement that causes the an increased heart rate

Page 110

gingerly - in a very careful way

Page 111

offence - anger, resentment or hurt

Page 116

traumatic - extremely distressing, frightening, or shocking

Page 117

perspective - a way of looking at things

exasperating - to make somebody very angry or frustrated

Page 118

figments - something only existing in somebody's imagination

Page 121

conjuring - the performance of magic tricks, making something appear

Page 124

profile - a level or degree of noticeability

Page 126

frequenting - to go to or be in a place often

Page 127

evade - to escape or avoid somebody or something

Page 133

immobilized - to prevent somebody or something from moving

preoccupied - completely absorbed in thinking about something or doing something, sometimes to the extent of neglecting other things

Page 134

decrepit - in poor condition, especially as a result of being old

Page 138

fending - to take care of somebody or something

Page 142

speculating - to guess based on incomplete facts or information

Page 145

orb - a sphere (ball shaped) or spherical object

Page 146

accosted - to approach and stop somebody, especially in an aggressive way

Page 150

prompted - to encourage someone to do something

Page 152

inconspicuous - not easily seen or noticed

Page 153

encountered - a brief, unexpected meeting with something

Page 157

truancy - staying away from school without permission

illuminated - to make visible with light

Page 166

irrelevant - not important

restraining - to keep somebody or something under control or within limits

Page 167

incapable - not being able to do something

Page 169

devastated - to shock or upset somebody greatly

traumatically - extremely distressing, frightening, or shocking

Page 171

ceremoniously - being careful to observe formalities and behave correctly

Page 174

reverted - to return to a former state

Page 175

elaborately - having many different parts or a lot of detail, and organized in a complicated way

Page 178

sceptical - not inclined to believe

Page 183

double-cross - turn a situation around to have an outcome other than what was expected

spectacularly - impressive or dramatic to look at or watch

Page 184

compass - a tool for drawing circles or measuring distance

yielded - to stop resisting

plume - a rising column of something such as smoke, dust, or water

Page 185

relish - to enjoy or take great pleasure in an experience

undistinguishable - impossible to tell apart from somebody or something else

Page 186

skein - a length of yarn or thread wound loosely and coiled together

Page 190

apprehensive - worried that something bad will happen

Page 191

syringes - needles

Page 193

instinct - a powerful impulse that feels natural rather than thought out

Page 196

repercussions - something, especially an unforeseen problem, that results from an action

Page 199

rookie - somebody who is new to an activity or job

constable - in the United Kingdom, Canada, Australia, and New Zealand, a police officer of the lowest rank

Page 200

anonymous - one whose name is not known or not given

accusations - a claim that somebody has done something illegal or wrong

Page 204

shimmery - to shine softly with a wavering or flickering light

Page 205

quavered - to tremble because of nervousness or fear

Page 210

consolation - a source of comfort to somebody who is upset or disappointed

Page 212

tactlessly - not concerned about upsetting or offending people

Page 216

implication - the state of suggesting something, without it being plainly expressed

intentionally - done on purpose, not by accident

Page 226

derelict - in poor condition because of neglect

Page 227

blood-curdling - arousing extreme fear

Page 228

trance - a state in which somebody is dazed or stunned or in some other way unaware of the environment

Page 230

threshold - a doorway or entrance

Page 233

epilogue - a short chapter or section at the end of a literary work, sometimes detailing the fate of its characters

exhumed - to dig up a corpse from a grave

coroner - a public official responsible for investigating deaths that appear not to have natural causes

trauma - a physical injury or wound to the body

campaigned - to take part in a drive to achieve a specific goal

Page 234

solemnly - having or showing no joy or humour

Page 237

insensitive - too little awareness of other people's feelings

Page 238

phantom - a ghost or apparition

ABOUT THE AUTHOR

Katherine Swanson is an author of children's books and novels, who currently resides in British Columbia, Canada.

She was born in Kenora, Ontario, Canada where she learned to love the outdoors and fine arts. After graduating from Lakehead University (Thunder Bay, Ontario), she moved to British Columbia to pursue a career in teaching.

Katherine wrote Guardian of the Ghost Key (her first novel) while on a leave of absence from teaching. She has continued to pursue her creative passion through novels, writing and illustrating children's picture books and poetry.

K. E. SWANSON

26309728R00163

Made in the USA
Charleston, SC
02 February 2014